A DISCARDED ROSE

A Novel

By

DAVIED E. KELLEY, JR.

PublishAmerica
Baltimore

© 2010 by Davied E. Kelley, Jr.
All rights reserved. No part of this book may be reproduced, stored in a retrieval system or transmitted in any form or by any means without the prior written permission of the publishers, except by a reviewer who may quote brief passages in a review to be printed in a newspaper, magazine or journal.

First printing

All characters in this book are fictitious, and any resemblance to real persons, living or dead, is coincidental.

PublishAmerica has allowed this work to remain exactly as the author intended, verbatim, without editorial input.

Hardcover 978-1-4560-2489-5
Softcover 978-1-4560-2490-1
PUBLISHED BY PUBLISHAMERICA, LLLP
www.publishamerica.com
Baltimore

Printed in the United States of America

ACKNOWLEDGEMENTS

    I would like to take the opportunity to thank everyone involve with this project. First, to Laura and Angie; two brazen volunteers. You were the first to read my, unedited, manuscript; not knowing where I was going to take you. Even after being subjected to my darker side, you both offered some sound advice and some very good criticism, which I needed in order to make this story more believable. I appreciate you both! Second, to Ridardian; what can I say, but WOW! Your cover concept is exactly what I envisioned. Thank you! Lastly, to my lovely wife for having to put up with the dark mood swings writing this story brought out of me. I love you. Thank you for your encouragement and patience, and love.

Innocence…
Once taken, it can never be returned.

PROLOGUE

It's Saturday afternoon, and the Pueblo Drive cul-de-sac is full of life; adults are busy doing weekend chores, while their children enjoy their free time playing. A game of tag quickly descends into a more violent form of dodge ball; but when little Ashley Patterson is hit in the face they stop throwing the ball at each other and decided to play hide-n-seek instead. But because no one wanted to be 'It', they decide to play a quick game of rock, paper, and scissors. The little boy that lost the game planted his face firmly against an oak tree. When he began to count the other children, giggling and laughing, scattered.

"One, two!" he begins, and then giggles, because he's confident he knows were all the good hiding places are located.

"Three...!"

Impulsively, the little boy leans his head back and looks up at the clouds. And forgetting momentarily what it was he was doing, he points toward the animal caricatures he recognizes in the sky.

"O-o-oh, a horsey!" he squealed, and then looks around to see if anyone else saw the horse.

"No fair!" someone shouts from their concealment, "he's cheating!"

When the little boy hears the cheating accusation, he immediately returns his head back against the tree, and to prove he's not cheating, he holds both his palms against the sides of his face.

"Four...Five! Ready or not, here I come!"

The little boy turns around, but he doesn't see anyone. Even the adults who were diligently working in their yards are gone.

"Hey, where'd y'all go?"

The little boy walks away from the tree and begins to meander through the other yards searching, until he finds himself standing in the middle of the street. Turning in circles, he eventually spots a pair of dirty sneakers that are concealed behind the unkempt row of hedges bordering the yard of the vacant house on the corner.

"I see you," he whispered and runs toward the hedges. But when the little boy burst through the hedges, he skids to a halt and falls backwards. The sneakers don't belong to any of his playmates. They instead belong to another boy; an older boy.

The older boy is holding a beer bottle in one hand, and a smoldering joint in the other. His eyes are red, and he's high.

"S'up kiddo?" he says, while puffing on the joint.

"Nothing," replied the little boy, as he gets up and dusts off his pants.

"Playing hide-n-seek, huh?"

"Uh-huh, and I'm 'It'."

"Of course you are."

The older boy's lips part to reveal a mouth full of stained, jagged teeth. They remind the little boy of the wolf in the Little Red Riding Hood story.

"Find anyone yet?" asks the older boy. He exhales, and blows the smoke out through his nose. Now the little boy thinks of dragons; the fire breathing kind.

"Naw…not yet, but I will!" he replies with confidence.

"I saw some of your friends," said the older boy. He tilts his head toward the old vacant house. "They went in there."

When the little boy looked pass the older boy, toward the house, he swallowed loudly.

"No they didn't."

The older boy, pretending he didn't care, shrugged and raised the joint to his lips again.

"Sure they did," he said, sounding like a hoarse dragon.

"Why would they go in there?"

"I don't know, maybe because they knew you won't. Or maybe because they know you're a sissy."

"I ain't a sissy!"

"Uh-huh," harrumphed the older boy, while drinking from the bottle.

"Well, I ain't!" insisted the little boy.

"Okay...no point getting all upset."

"I ain't upset."

A gush of wind blew over the top of the hedges, and when it reached the old house, it rattled the broken glass in one of the windows. The little boy reacted to the sound by looking in the direction of the noise, where he saw a tattered piece of drapery move.

The older boy, taking advantage of the distraction, tossed his empty beer bottle over the back of his head. It landed on the house's porch with an ear shattering crash.

"Hear that?" he said, "they're in there laughing at you!"

"No they ain't!"

The older boy pressed one finger against his mouth and shushed the little boy, telling him to be quiet. Then he cupped one hand behind his ear and pretended he heard giggling.

"Can't you hear them?"

"That's just the wind," answered the little boy, displaying fake bravado.

"Hey, it's okay if you're too scared to go in there. Hell I was scared too, the first time I went in there."

"Really, you...scared?"

"Well...yeah!" exclaimed the older boy and he turned toward the house.

"It is a scary place, ain't it?" he adds while staring at the house. "But once I got over how it looked, everything was okay."

"You weren't scared?"

"Naw...com'on, I'll show you."

The older boy reached for the little boy's hand. He took one step forward, but once he realized he had stepped out into the open, he withdrew it and then looked up and down the street; to see if anyone had seen him talking to the little boy.

"What's wrong?" asked the little boy, but the older boy didn't respond. Instead, he grabbed the little boy by the hand and walked toward the house.

"Oh, nothing…nothing at all," he answered.

# # #

1

A shiny sedan comes to a stop next to the curb in front of two working girls loitering on the sidewalk. The smiling black man, sitting behind the steering wheel, beckons for one of them to come over.

When Cecilia sees the john, she gestures to Rosie, with a slight tilt of her head, and tells her to go find out what he wants.

"¿Usted que va a tomar éste, o qué?" she says, speaking in her native language, but Rosie doesn't move.

"Naw, CC…Let's pass on this one. He looks like a cop to me. Besides, you know I don't like the *really* black ones."

"What the fuck's wrong with you?" asked Cecilia. She pushes away from the wall she's leaning against, and goes out to the car. When she bends to look inside the wind catches her short skirt and lifts it up; revealing her bare ass. But having been stripped of her dignity a long time ago, Cecilia ignores the over exposure.

"¿Usted que va a tomar éste, o qué?" she asks, and the driver replies with, "You open for business, 'cause if you are, I need to make a deposit?"

Cecilia stepped away from the car, and waved dismissively with a flip of her hand.

"Man, this ain't a bank! Go on! Get out 'a here, before you get us busted!"

"Aw' com'on sweet thang," pleads the john, "Let me take that *fine* ass of yours for a test ride. Hell, if you're game, I'll take on you and your pretty little friend over there."

Cecilia glanced back and looked down the street, searching for another, more suitable, customer. When she didn't see one, she reconsidered the black man's offer and leans down; into the window. Boldly, she grabs hold of his crotch.

"You ain't the po'po, are you? Cause if you are, you ain't supposed to let me do this. That's entrapment."

"I ain't a cop," replied the john, and to prove his point, he sticks his hand into his shirt pocket and pulls out a wad of twenty-dollar bills, and waves it in the air.

"Com'on, why don't you go get your friend and let's party!"

Cecilia stepped back from the car. Smiling, she walked over to where Rosie was standing and whispered in her ear.

Initially, Rosie didn't respond. But when she looked at the black man sitting in the car, she shook her head.

"Uh-uh…I got a bad feeling about this one, CC."

Cecilia, angry and determined, grabbed Rosie by her forearm, and pulled her toward the waiting customer.

"Com'on bitch, our rents late, now get your ass in gear and let's make this money!"

Cecilia dragged Rosie to the car and opened the back door. After shoving Rosie into the back seat, she slammed the door, and then got into the front passenger seat.

"Sugar," she said, when she faced the john. "You got yourself two *hot* Latina sisters, so I hope you can afford it."

The john, eager to get started, slammed his foot down on the accelerator and sped away from the curb.

"Got a place close by, maybe a hotel room?" he asked, but Cecilia ignored his question and pointed toward an upcoming traffic light.

"Turn left here, and then head to Jones Street. When you get there, make a left and keep driving, 'til you see the truck entrance leading to the back of the convention center."

"Is it safe there?"

"Com'on man, be for real, we're not thieves."

Cecilia re-positioned herself in the seat and pulled her knees up against her chest, so the john could see what he was about to purchase.

"But you can spank me, like I stole something, if you want," she said, and the john, mesmerized by the sight of Cecilia's beautiful body, took one hand off his steering wheel and reached out to touch Cecilia. When she saw him do that, Cecilia wagged her finger at him and put down her legs.

"Uh-uh…Look-sees are free. If you want to touch, we need to be paid first."

The john, excited and anxious, reached for his shirt pocket again. He pulled out the wad of money he had flashed earlier, and without counting it, handed it all to Cecilia.

"That enough?" he asked.

"Yeah…for starters," replied Cecilia, while flipping through the cash.

"Is this the place?" he asked, when he spots the guard shack. He slows and hesitating, looks cautiously around.

"You've used this place before?"

"Yeah, all the time." answers Rosie, finally speaking up.

"What about the guard? Where's he? Ain't he gonna stop us from going down there?"

"Don't worry 'bout him," answered Rosie.

"Well…Okay, if you're sure?"

"I'm sure…just drive," replied Rosie, sounding irritated.

After the john made the turn, he rushed pass the empty guard shack without slowing. At the end of the road, he saw trailers; dozens of them and they were all backed against the docks. Rosie leaned forward, and from the back seat, pointed toward an empty space between two trailers.

"Over there, where it's nice and dark!"

"Yeah, nice and dark…" repeated the john, "just the way I like it."

# # #

2

Dreams…

Everyone has dreams and Daniel is no different in that regard; except he keeps having the same dream, over and over. In fact, he's had the same one so often, and for so long, he can't remember when it first began. Or why the ghostly little boy in it haunts him.

A phone rings.

Daniel hears the ringing, and wonders what the significance of it is, but he doesn't turn away from the little boy.

The ringing gets louder.

When Daniel looks at the phone, he sees it lying on the ground nestled in a bed of beautiful red roses. He reached for it, but the phone suddenly sprouts legs and scurries away. Startled by the sight of a walking phone, Daniel's eyes pop open and he looks up at the rotating ceiling fan hanging from the ceiling.

The ringing gets louder as if the phone is insisting it be answered.

Daniel turns slowly away from the ceiling fan, and looks to his left. He sees his cell phone lying on his nightstand. The face of it is lit up, but there are no legs sticking out of its side, and it's not moving. So he sits up and wipes the sleep from his eyes.

"Okay," he moaned, reaching for the phone.

"What'cha got?" he groaned, without a greeting, and the caller said, "You have an active crime scene, detective."

The caller's voice was familiar, but it commanded respect, because it belonged to Captain Peterson, Daniel's boss and father-in-law.

Daniel looked for the clock, but when he didn't see the time, he picked it up. It had been lying face down.

"Jesus...Three a.m.," he groaned softly when he saw the time, and the captain heard him.

"You wanted to be a detective, didn't you? So get your ass up, and get over to that crime scene pronto, before the news cameras beat you to it!"

"Okay, cap...I'll be there in thirty, just make sure the scene is secured. I don't want anyone disturbing it, 'til I get there."

Daniel yawned while listening to the captain's reaction to his demands, and in response to something the captain said, he vigorously shook his head.

"No!" he said, elevating his voice. "They can collect their forensic specimens *after* I've seen it in its native state!"

Lowering his voice, Daniel added, "Captain, please? You know that's how my mind works."

The captain started his customary ranting and ravings, so Daniel pulled the phone away from his ear. While waiting for the tirade to stop, he looked over at Louise. She hadn't moved, so he placed the phone against his ear and said good-bye. Without waiting to hear the captain's reply, Daniel flipped the phone shut and sat it down. He tossed back his bed covers and threw his feet over the side of the bed, but he paused, when Louise spoke.

"Where are you going babe?" she asked. Apparently, she had been awaken by the phone's insistent ringing and had heard the entire conversation between Daniel and her father.

"Got 'a go to work baby," answered Daniel, "Go back to sleep."

"But—" Louise sat up and rubbed her eyes. "—what's so important it can't wait 'til morning?"

Daniel turned toward the window and saw the moon. *The sun will be up soon*, he thought.

"It is morning and besides—"

Walking over to his dresser, Daniel pulled open the top drawer. He pulled a metal box out of the drawer, and after sitting it on top of the dresser, spun the three digit combination lock. When he opened the box,

Daniel picked up his service revolver and pulled back the slide bar; to make sure he had not left a bullet chambered when he put it away.

"—it's my job, so I have to respond. You know that."

"But—" Louise pouted. She raised her arms and gestured for Daniel to come near. "—I was hoping for some morning loving."

Daniel stared through the darkness and looked at the sexy lingerie Louise wore. One of her boobs was exposed—the strap had slipped off her shoulder during the night—and the sight of it excited him. They had made love that night, but he found he still lusted after her. So, giving in to his desires, Daniel stepped closer to the bed and bent to kiss Louise, but once he was close enough, she grabbed him by his neck and pulled him back into the bed.

"Honey, I've got to go!"

"Oh, com'on, don't tell me you don't want it? I'll make it worth your while."

"Okay, but it has to be a quickie."

"That's all I need…"

# # #

3

Rush hour always starts early in Atlanta, and today is no different. So when Daniel reaches the back up, he turns on his siren and blue lights and moves over into I-75's emergency lane. There, he speeds pass the congestion, until he comes to the *Techwood Avenue* exit. He turns off his siren, and with his lights still on, drives toward Centennial Park. When he begins to smell the pungent fish odor coming from the new aquarium, Daniel knows he's close to his destination. He turns right at *Marietta Street* and heads toward *Jones Street*, where he knows it will take him directly to *North Side Drive*, and on to the far side of the Congress Center. As he nears the convention zone, Daniel notices the bronze historical marker along side the street. It's there so curious tourist can read and learn more about the history of the neighborhood the Congress Center facility sits.

Once known as Mechanicsville, the neighborhood was considered the hood, because it was populated by poor white trash and the descendents of slaves. Annexed by Atlanta's city fathers in the early seventies, the convention center was built to rival New York's Jacob Javit Center and Chicago's McCormick Place. Once it was completed, the surrounding property, long envied by developers, was condemned by the city and sold. And the next thing you know, Atlanta's inner city is no longer a blithe on the landscape. Instead, it's now an upscale urban neighborhood which only the rich can afford—just like New York and Chicago. When the crime rate in the area increased, specifically those crimes involving tourist and conventioneers, no one originally from the area was surprised, because after all, the area was still technically *'the hood'*. The criminals didn't move away, like the other poor residents who were forced out. Instead, they just waited, and like alligators waiting for wildebeests to cross the river, they began to pick off the unsuspecting tourist and conventioneers.

When Daniel turned on Northside Drive, he passed the front of the Congress Center, with its towering castle-like façade of stonewalls and pillars. Looking up at it, he wondered why no one had thought to add an alligator moat, or a draw bride, to complete the medieval appearance of the convention center. After passing by the guard shack, Daniel took notice and saw it was dark. No one was manning the station, and as plain as day, he saw the gate was broken.

Daniel drove down the access road that separated *'B'* and *'C'* building, and when the lights from his cruiser illuminated it; the road reminded him of a lunar landscape, with its crater-size potholes. A television news truck was parked off to the side, next to *'C'* building and directly across from the crime scene.

"Vultures," mumbled Daniel, when the news cameraman swung the camera on him.

Police cruisers, and a forensic van, were parked in the middle of the road, blocking the camera man's view. The blue and white lights flashing from the top of the cruisers created eerie montages of dancing shadows against the sides of the building, while the yellow crime scene tape flapped violently against the morning breeze. When Daniel got out of his car, he immediately heard the sound they made and thought they sounded like far off war drums, which emphasized the effect of the dancing shadows.

Daniel approached the crime scene tape and grabbed it with one hand. He raised it chest high, before ducking beneath it and walking over to the officer who had initially responded to the call. But the officer, busy completing his report, didn't acknowledge him or look up. Instead, he gestured over his shoulder with his thumb and pointed toward the crime scene.

"Over there. It's a good kill," he mumbled, meaning it was bad...*really* bad.

"Why's that thing running?" Daniel asked, pointing toward one of the forklifts. When the officer didn't respond, Daniel elevated his voice and said, "Hey! I asked you a question."

The officer looked up, and Daniel saw the dark circles around his eyes. He knew the man was tired, but that was no excuse for his lack of decorum.

"Huh, you say something?" the officer yawned.

"Yes, why's that thing still running?" answered Daniel speaking in a softer tone, after deciding to cut the officer some slack.

The officer released an audible sigh. His shift was nearly over and all he wanted to do was finish his report, so he could turn the crime scene over to the detective.

"It was running when I got here, and my orders were not to touch anything, which is why it's still running."

Daniel thought of the conversation he had had with Captain Peterson. Obviously, the captain had heard his request and conveyed it to the officer.

"Where are the Vic's" he asked, while pulling a pin light out of his coat pocket. He shined the light on the forklift, but he didn't see any blood, or signs of foul play, so he spun around and faced the officer again.

The officer raised his larger flashlight and illuminated the entire front of the forklift, so Daniel could see the two bodies hanging from its blades.

Daniel walked around the forklift and stepped up to the bodies. He grabbed one by the hair and raised its head, and could see it was a woman. Blood rushed from the wound in her neck and splattered on the ground.

"Think you can find someone to move this thing back a few feet?" asked Daniel, of the officer, while continuing his cursory examination of the victim. But when no immediate response came, he looked back at the officer.

"Hey? You hard of hearing, I'm talking to you!"

"Jesus…detective, it's four in the morning! Who am I gonna get to move that thing?"

"I don't know…find someone."

The officer, angry, stormed toward his cruiser. While Daniel, thinking he was going to get in his car and leave, stood there holding onto the victim's hair.

"Hey—" he called out, but when the officer went to the passenger side of his cruiser, instead of the driver's side, Daniel shut his mouth. He observed while the officer opened the door and angrily tossed in his clipboard. When he turned, and walked back to the forklift, Daniel asked, "What are you doing?"

"You want it moved, don't 'cha?" asked the officer, with one foot on the forklift's sidestep, preparing to climb aboard it.

"You know how to operate it?"

"Yeah…," answered the officer as he reached for the steering wheel. "I used to work here part-time, while I attended the academy."

"Then can you move it without smudging those prints?"

"Huh?"

Daniel raised his pin light and pointed toward the steering wheel. When the officer looked at it, he saw the smudged fingerprints too. He hadn't seen them before.

"Yeah…Sure…why not?"

#

Once the officer had finished moving the forklift, he jumped off it and walked back to where Daniel was standing, staring at the bodies.

"Crack ho's?" he asked, but Daniel shook his head, disagreeing.

"Naw…don't think so."

There was something lying on the ground, so Daniel walked away from the officer and picked it up. It was a small clutch purse.

"Hookers maybe…" he added, "Crack ho's don't carry expensive stuff like this."

While he checked the purse for ID, Daniel noticed something else on the ground, beneath one of the bodies.

"Grab that, will you, and that…" he said, pointing at something just outside the shadow of the light. "What is that, a rose?"

The officer turned his flashlight toward the spot where Daniel had indicated and saw another purse, and a flower. They were both lying beneath the bodies.

"Aw, Jesus…Detective! It's covered in blood."

Daniel looked up from the purse he has and points toward the other on the ground.

"Go on," he insists.

Reluctantly, the officer walked around the dangling bodies and kneels. He picks up the purse and rose, but before standing, looks into the face of one of the victims.

"This one's a real looker," he says. When he looks pass the bodies, to Daniel, he sees him staring down at the driver's license he has found.

"Huh?" Daniel says and looks up. "You say something?"

"I said, 'This one's a real looker.'" repeated the officer, as he approached Daniel. Once he arrives back to where Daniel is standing, Daniel snatched the purse.

"Give me that!" he said, and quickly opened it. Once he locates the wallet, and opens it, Daniel winces painfully. "Damn."

"What? You know these girls?"

Daniel looked up from the license to the officer. Using his pin light, he points to the first body and then the second.

"That's Cecilia Garcia and that's her baby sister, Rosie."

#

Standing outside her van, waiting patiently, was APD Forensic Team Leader Becky Randall. When Daniel saw her; he raised his hand and signaled for her, and her crew, to enter the crime scene.

"I want a full work up on them, okay?" he said, growling.

When Becky walked up to Daniel, she was about to lodge a complaint about being held back from the crime scene, but Daniel looked away from her and said, "Blood work, DNA, Rape kit...The works, understand?" When he turned to face Becky, she nodded, but didn't say anything.

"These were good girls, and they didn't deserve to die this way." Daniel sadly added.

Becky was just about to tell Daniel to step back, so her team could do their job, but she decided against saying that after detecting the emotion in Daniel's voice.

"You know these girls?" she instead asked.

"Yeah..." Daniel nodded.

"Sorry to hear that." Becky walked pass Daniel. "I'll call you as soon as I'm done. Good enough?"

Daniel, without replying, steps aside and walks away. He looks around the crime scene as if he's searching for someone.

"Where is that goddamn security guard?" he barks, speaking to no one person in particular. But a man, that had been standing among the police officers, joking and laughing, responds. He is tall, and rail thin, and he's dressed in a uniform that closely resembles an Atlanta police officer's.

"How can I help?"

Daniel walked up to the guard and grabs him by the arm. He escorts him away from the gathering of policemen. After they are several yards away, Daniel stops walking, and he turns to face the guard.

"I need to know who has access to the forklifts keys after hours."

The upset emotion on Daniel's face is obvious, so the guard gets serious and answers matter-of-factly.

"No one uses them after hours," he replies.

"Where are the keys maintained? Aren't they supposed to be locked in a key box, or something?"

"Well...yeah, I reckon there's a lock box 'round hea' somewhere, but it ain't my job to monitor their use. 'Sides ain't nobody works 'round hea' this time of the morning no how."

"Then how do you explain what happened over there?"

Daniel points toward crime scene, but the guard just shrugs. His demeanor is detached and it is obvious to Daniel he doesn't care.

"I don't know," he answers.

Daniel points toward the empty guard shack without taking his eyes off the guard, because as far as he's concerned, he was a suspect too.

"Isn't someone supposed to be stationed there to prevent people from wondering in back here?"

"Yeah…So?"

"So? So?"

Daniel clinched his teeth, and trying to control his raging emotions, stepped uncomfortably close to the guard. The guard stepped back.

"Then why ain't it locked?" he barked, and spittle flew from his mouth toward the guard.

"Cause, the gate's broken—" the guard replied with an elevated voice, but he quickly lowered it; in deference to Daniel's authority. He wiped his cheek and said, "—and maintenance 'round this hea' place ain't my job either. Look officer—"

Daniel held up one finger and immediately silenced the guard.

"It's detective," he said to him.

"Huh? What?"

"I'm a Detective—"

Daniel opened his trench coat to allow the guard a glimpse of his detective's shield and gun. It was strapped beneath his shoulder, while the shield was clipped to his belt.

"—Detective Rose," said Daniel.

"Okay, De…tec…tive—" the guard added emphasis to each syllable of the word.

"You being a smart ass, because if that's the case, you should know, I ain't the one to be fucking with?"

"No…look," answered the guard, "What I am trying to say is; people come back here all the time."

"People…what people?"

"Hookers and their johns…I got tired of running them off every night, 'cause they always come back. Reported it to my boss, and he told me to stop patrolling back here. Said, since the whores weren't actually trying to break into the place, there was no need risking my neck chasing them off."

"Then why were you here tonight?"

Daniel leaned forward—so close he could smell salami and onions on the guard's breathe—and asked, "Were you cruising for a piece of ass?"

When he winked a rush of indignation overcame the guard and he blurted, "What? Sir, I'm a married man!"

The other policemen standing around heard the guard's loud response and looked in his direction. When Daniel realized he had attracted their attention, he tried to calm down the guard.

"Okay, okay…" he said to him. "You're faithful. I get it. Don't go getting your panties bunched up into a wad."

"You should show more respect."

"Okay, I get it! Now tell me, why were you here?"

"Cause I heard noises, and decided to investigate. That's what they pay me for."

The guard raised the large yellow flashlight he was holding, and when he turned it on, it illuminated the entire far end of the building.

"I was standing there when I heard the forklift cranking."

"And what time was that?"

Daniel had pulled out a leather bound notebook from his pocket, and was scribbling in it.

"'About Two thirty, I guess."

"What happen next?"

The guard swung his light around, and pointed toward the other end of the building, where the crime scene was.

"I saw a man sitting there, on that forklift. When he saw me, he jumped off of it and ran."

"Ran…which way?"

"Down the access road, pass the guard shack."

Daniel looked up from the notepad and stared at the guard for a moment.

"You mean the one with the broken gate?" he asked, and the guard nodded slowly, because it had just occurred to him; he had let the killer escape.

"I'm in trouble, ain't I?"

"Naw, you ain't in any trouble," answered Daniel, while closing his note book. He stuffed it back into his pocket and turning, walked away.

"But if I were you," he added, calling back over his shoulder. "I'd start looking for another line of work, because you suck at this!"

"Detective Rose!" a reporter, seeing an opening, shouted from the side of the road. "What happened here tonight?"

"No comment!" yelled Daniel as he made his way toward his car.

Once he had sat down in the quiet confines of the car, Daniel pulled out the two driver's licenses and stared at them.

# # #

4

"*¡hola muchachos!*" two girls shout. When Daniel and Saul saw them, wearing nothing but revealing bikini swimsuits, Daniel is reminded of the sirens in *Homer's Odyssey* that lured sailors to there death. Still, they stop and approached the fence surrounding the house.

"*¡Usted está pareciendo bueno hoy!*" shouts Cecilia. She sits up and waves.

"What's she saying?" Saul asks Daniel, because he doesn't understand Spanish.

"They think we're hot," answered Daniel, and then, speaking directly to Cecilia, he said, "*¿Cuál está...para arriba?*"

Cecilia giggled, because Daniel's Spanish is awkward and clumsy. But then she replies and says, "*Dé vuelta alrededor, así que puedo ver ese asno fino el suyo!*"

In response to Cecilia, Daniel turns around and lifts his shirt, so she could see his butt.

"What's going on? Why are you doing that?" asked Saul, clearly irritated by the private conversation going on between the Mexican siren and his friend, Daniel.

Daniel didn't answer, because if Saul knew what he was doing, and why, Daniel knew he'd never live it down. So instead, he shrugged and grinning sheepishly shook his but for the girls.

"*Que' acerca de los negro uno, a?*" said Cecilia, whispering into her sister's ear. Rosie, rejecting the idea, answered in English.

"You know I don't like the black ones," she said, and Saul heard her.

"What the hell's that 'pose to mean?" he asked, looking to Daniel for an answer. "Just what the hell's going on? They been talking 'bout me all along?"

"Naw," answered Daniel, truthfully, but Saul didn't believe him.

"Then what are they talking 'bout?" he asked.

"Nothing…they just fooling around, that's all."

"You think we're fooling, huh?" asked Cecilia, when she over heard Daniel.

Daniel, still facing Saul, glanced passed him and looked at Cecilia. She parted her legs quickly and flashed her *goodies.*

"¿Para mí, seria mente?" asked Daniel, and Cecilia nodded. She winked too, and licked her tongue sensuously over her lips.

"Serious?" asked Daniel, excited.

Saul turned in time to see what Cecilia was doing, and thinking they were still talking about him, shouted, "S'hey bitch!" Then he grabbed his crotch and hunched suggestively.

"Ain't anybody talking to' yo' rusty black ass, Saul!" snapped Cecilia, but just as quickly, she returned her attention back to Daniel.

"We're talking to Danny boy," she said, sweetly.

"Hey, fuck you bitch!"

"Cool it, will ya?" said Daniel, holding up one hand, but Saul ignored him. And continuing to antagonize the girls, he held his fingers up to his mouth and licked his tongue out between them.

"Eeew!" exclaimed the girls, disgusted by the sight of Saul's cherry red tongue.

"Come on man," Saul said, turning away from the girls. He looked at Daniel. "Let's go to the park and play ball."

Daniel didn't move.

"Com'on," insisted Saul as he took a few steps, "the guys are waiting for us."

"Naw, I think I'm gonna hang out for a while. See what's up."

"You can't be for real? Daniel, they ain't serious."

Saul looked pass Daniel and stared at Rosie. She had turned over and was now lying on her stomach. Of the two sisters, she was the one

Saul was attracted to, but the Latin beauty had made it clear; he wasn't her type.

"They're just yanking your chain," Saul added, once he tore his eyes away from Rosie's butt. "Com'on, let's go."

"Saul, I'll catch up with you later, man. Okay?"

"Danny—man, they just fucking 'round, 'cause they ain't got nothing better to do."

While talking, Saul was standing with his back to the girls and didn't see Rosie, when she inserted Cecilia's finger into her mouth and mimicked giving a blowjob.

"Uh, Saul..." Daniel said, and grabbing Saul by his shoulders, he ushered him toward the park. "Look, you go on. I'll catch up with you later."

"Whatever," mumbled Saul, and he walked away.

Daniel watched Saul for a moment. He had thought about leaving too, but when a pebble hit the back of his head, he turned around to find Cecilia standing behind him. Without warning, she reached out and fearlessly grabbed his crotch.

"Oh my!" she exclaimed, and withdrew her hand.

"What's wrong?"

Rosie had leapt to her feet and rushed out of the yard. Cecilia turned and looked at her with an unbelievably excited expression on her face.

"It's...It's gi-normous!"

Cecilia backed away from Daniel, and when Rosie came closer, she urged her forward.

"Go on...feel for your self," she said, but Rosie was not as audacious as her older sister. Still, at Cecilia's urging, she extended her hand and gently poked Daniel's crotch with one finger. But it didn't seem unusual, or so she thought, and she decided to give it a squeeze. Once she took in into her small hand and squeezed it, she yanked her hand back.

"Oh—my—god!" blurted Rosie, as she moved back to behind her older sister; where she coward nervously.

"What if it's too big?" she asked, and Cecilia, never considering the possibility, stepped forward again and touched Daniel's crotch once more; trying to determine just how big it really was.

"Ain't no such thing as *too* big," she said; still seductively staring into Daniel's eyes. She smiled. "Can you come over tonight, big boy? Our momma's working the late shift, and we'll be all alone and unprotected."

"Yeah, but—" replied Daniel, but before he could finish his statement, the two promiscuous girls turned and dashed back into their house.

"—I can't, until after my parents go to bed."

Daniel entered the Garcia house through an open back door. After he stepped inside the door slammed shut. He spun around and discovered Cecilia standing behind the door. She was wet, and wrapped in a towel.

"Follow me!" squealed Cecilia as she bolted passed Daniel and headed toward the stairs. When she reached the top of them, Cecilia dropped her towel, so Daniel could see her bare ass.

"Man, oh man!" exclaimed Daniel in a whisper. "Wait 'til the boys hear 'bout this."

When he neared the top of the stairs, Daniel thought he heard moaning, so he crept down the hall and to the master bedroom, where he peeked inside to find Rosie sprawled out on a king sized bed. Cecilia was down on her knees in front of her.

Rosie saw Daniel standing in the doorway, so she tapped Cecilia's shoulder to alert her of his presence. Cecilia looked back at Daniel. She stuck out her tongue, so he could see she was probing Rosie. When she finished, Cecilia stood and faced Daniel. She was standing there, completely naked, but Daniel couldn't help but notice the satisfied look on her face.

When Daniel didn't move, or react to what she had done, Cecilia walked over and took hold of his hand. It was trembling, so thinking she could help him relax, Cecilia placed it on one of her breast. When Daniel didn't react, she grabbed the hair on the back of his head and yanked it back, and then she kissed him. The budding nymph probed Daniel with an experienced tongue. After withdrawing it, she licked her lips and moaned, "Mmmm, you taste good!"

"Hey, don't hog him!" cried Rosie, when she saw the satiated look on Cecilia's face.

Cecilia looked back over her shoulder and winked at Rosie. Then without warning, she spun Daniel around and pushed him backwards.

"Hey!" yelped Daniel, but before he could right himself, Rosie pounced on top of him and ripped open his shirt. Buttons flew everywhere. She quickly unbuckled his belt too and when she opened his pants, and saw his rising manhood, she squealed gleefully.

When Cecilia saw Daniel's erection, she pushed her sister aside and selfishly positioned herself over it.

"Oh…my…god!" she cried, as she slowly began to hump up and down.

"C'mon CC, you swore you'd let me go first this time."

"I will—ugh—next time—AAAAAAH!"

Cecilia's orgasm came quickly, and it was so powerful it made her body shake. When she opened her eyes, Cecilia saw the disappointed look on Rosie's face. She bit down on her lip, and beckoned for Rosie to come closer.

"He ain't using his mouth, is he?" asked Cecilia, after kissing Rosie.

Daniel heard the girls whispering, so he opened his eyes and looked up, just in time to see Rosie positioning herself over his face. Inexperienced with sex, and the myriad ways a woman could be pleasured, Daniel didn't truthfully understand what it was he was supposed to do.

"Wait! I don't know—" he blurted, but Rosie sat down on his face and began to grind slowly back and forth.

"Yeah…right there. Ooooh!" cried Rosie, when Daniel's inexperienced tongue began to probe her

However, Daniel was naïve and thought he was supposed to mimic *actual* eating, which is what he did.

"Ouch! Wait! No! Don't bite!"

Rosie rose up, off Daniel's face, and waited for the pain to subside. Once it faded, she lowered her hips again.

"Ah-h-h...yeah baby, that's it, much better!"

Synchronizing her movements to match Daniel's inexperienced tongue, Rosie rocked slowly. When she feels the tingling of an orgasm, she speeds up her pace, while at the same time, encourages Daniel using a soft seductive tone.

"Com'on baby...that's it!" she moans, until her voice matched the strength of her approaching orgasm.

"Yeah, right there! Right there! Yeah! Yeah! Yeah! That's it, don't stop! Com'on! Com'on! AAAAAAAGH!"

After having had their way with Daniel, the Garcia girls politely tell him to leave. It was four A. M., and they were afraid their mother would come home early.

"I understand," Daniel says, and swings his legs off the side of the bed. "I got'ta get home anyway. My parents are early risers."

"Don't you tell," said Rosie, and Daniel glanced over his shoulder to get one more quick glimpse of her butt, just before she covers herself with the bed comforter.

"Never know," she adds, "we might invite you over again."

Cecilia crawled under the cover, and snuggled up next to Rosie.

"Make sure you lock the door when you leave," she said, yawning.

Daniel smiled, when he sees Cecilia nibbling on Rosie's ear lobe. He suspects they're going to do *it* again, after he's gone.

High school dances are always awkward, even for the most popular student, but when Daniel walked into the gym this time, he did so with the confidence of a boy who just became a man. After paying the door fee, he stepped in, but stopped just inside the door, to survey the landscape of pubescent adolescents who were pretending to be older, although no one was mature enough to ask anyone to dance. Instead, the children stood along side the outside boundary line of the basketball court, huddled in their peer groups.

The girls stood on the far side of the gym, but they were all broken down into subgroups; older girls; tweens; and the younger girls who were gathered next to the DJ's table, gawking at the high school senior that had volunteered to MC the dance. On the other side of the gym were the boys. They had their own form of hierarchy too. Standing further away from the gym's entrance, across from the older girls, stood the jocks. They all wore blazers and ties, trying to impress the girls. Next to them, but not too close, stood the intellectuals and jock wanna-be's. Although the intellectuals were smarter than the jocks, they envied them, because of their strength and physical prowess. To them the jocks were gods and someone to physically aspire to be. The wanna-be's just wanted to be part of the '*in crowd*', so they didn't care which group they stood next to, just as long as they were seen.

Gathered further down the male hierarchy were the loners, losers, and bullies. Saul was among them, but he stood alone, because he was a bully and no one dared approach him. But when Daniel saw him, he strutted over and quietly, stood next to him; smiling like a Cheshire cat.

"Why are you so happy?"

"Oh, I don't know. Just feeling good about myself, I guess."

Rosie and Cecilia were attending the dance too, and like all of the other girls, they stood on the opposite side of the gym gossiping. When Daniel saw them, he grinned knowingly.

"Hey, you remember the other day?" he asked Saul, but he was ignored. Saul was too busy watching the young girls standing next to the DJ's table.

"Huh? No, why, what happened?"

"You know...the other day, on La Vista Street?"

Saul didn't remember, so he shrugged.

"C'mon, man..." insisted Daniel, "you know...*thee* other day! The day we stopped to talk to the Garcia girls. Don't you remember that?"

Daniel looked at Saul and thought he looked like a hungry predator, sizing up his next kill.

"What the hell are you talking 'bout?" asked Saul, when he finally looked away from the girls and to Daniel.

Daniel raised his hand and quickly pointed toward the other side of the gym, and at Rosie and Cecilia.

"I hit that," he boasted.

"Hit what?"

Saul looked across the deserted dance floor, through the glare of the strobe lights, toward the group of older girls, but he didn't know which Daniel was referring to.

"Who?" he asked, and Daniel, forgetting his promise not to tell, pointed directly at Rosie and Cecilia.

"Them."

"What?" Saul turned to face Daniel. "Bull shit. You're lying."

Saul looking back across the gym and stared at the sisters. When he looked back at Daniel, he thought, *anyone could get lucky, even Daniel.*

"Okay, I'll bite..." he said, "which one?"

"That's just it; I screwed 'em both...and at the same time!"

Saul's mouth dropped open.

"What?"

"And let me tell you..." continued Daniel, oblivious to Saul's envy. "Those bitches are real freaks."

"They are?"

"Yeah...when I first walked into their house, Cecilia greeted me at the door wearing nothing but a smile."

"No shit, serious?"

"Seriously...and when I got up to their mother's bedroom, they let me watch, while they ate out each other."

Saul turned green with envy, although you couldn't see it because of his dark skin. He turned away from Daniel and stared across the dance floor.

Why would they put out for him, and not me? What, because I'm too black? What kind of reason is that?

Saul stared longingly at Rosie. He licked his lips and clinched his fist, growing angrier by the second.

Look at her, pretending to be a virgin.

When Rosie moved, and mingled with the crowd, Saul followed her every step. As his eyes surveyed every inch of her body, Saul envied the sun dress she wore; how it caressed her form and emphasized her curves. He yearned to be the dress, and imagined himself flowing down her back, like water, over her apple bottom shaped butt.

Rosie sensed someone's burning stare, so she stopped talking and turn to face the empty dance floor. She held her hand over her eyes, to shadow the glare coming from the strobe light, and saw Saul. He was standing there, with his hand in his pocket, playing pocket pool.

Is he looking at me, and what's he doing in his pocket?

"Ugh, that's disgusting!" exclaimed Rosie, once she realized what it was Saul was doing. She backed away from the edge of the crowd and moved deep into the group, until she was sure she had faded into the crowd.

Realizing he had been found out, Saul whipped his head aside and pretended to be looking elsewhere.

Is he looking at me?

When Saul looked back across the gym, he couldn't find Rosie, so he turned back to Daniel.

"I don't believe you," he said.

"Look man, I'm telling you...I spanked that ass nearly all night long. And I would have done it all night too, if they weren't afraid their mother would come home early. She works the night shift on Wednesdays and Fridays."

"So...that means she's working tonight, huh?"

The predatory appearance returned to Saul's face as his eyes narrowed. He grinned and it appeared as though his canine teeth elongated into fangs.

"Yeah, but don't say anything, okay?" asked Daniel, realizing he had spilled the beans. "Or they won't let me come over again."

Saul nodded. He turned and faced the dance floor again. With one hand still in his pocket, he stuck his finger back into the hole at the bottom of it and resumed fondling his pecker.

"Don't worry…I got'cha back," he said, unconvincingly. "Besides, ain't nobody gonna believe it no how."

"I swear…I ain't lying."

"Really…then prove it."

Saul pulled his hand out of his pocket and sniffed it, not caring that Daniel knew what he had been doing. Squinting, he searched the crowd, opposite of where they were standing, until he spots Rosie.

"Go ask her to dance," he says, "and if she does, I'll believe you. But if she don't I'll tell everyone you're full of shit."

Daniel gazed nervously across the gym floor, at Rosie. She was standing with a group of older girls.

"Dance?" he asked, gulping down the word.

"Yeah…You *can* dance, can't you?"

Daniel doesn't reply. Instead, he accepts the challenge and steps out and onto the empty dance floor.

#

Rosie was standing with the group of older girls; talking and enjoying herself, until Daniel tapped her shoulder.

"Hey, how's it going?"

"I'm sorry, do I know you?" replied Rosie, pretending she didn't know Daniel.

Daniel saw the petrified look on Rosie's face, and when he glanced passed her and toward the other girls, he thought he understood why. So he winked and decided to play on.

"Oh, I get it!"

"Get what? Who are you, and what do you want?"

"To dance," answered Daniel, with his hand out, but Rosie didn't take it. Instead, she pretended to be surprised.

"What—me—dance with you?"

The girls behind Rosie began to laugh and snicker, so she joined in.

"He wants to dance with me," she laughed and walked away.

#

The following day, Daniel found himself walking down the street toward Rosie's house. He was angry, and wanted to know why she acted as though she didn't know him. But when he arrived there, and found Rosie standing by the fence, he was puzzled. Apparently, she wanted to talk to him too.

"Last night you made a fool out'ta me," said Daniel the moment he stepped up to the fence.

"Well, you deserved it."

"I don't get it. A couple nights ago, you couldn't keep your hands off me, but last night, you gave me the cold shoulder. What's up with that?"

"Boys…You don't know anything."

Rosie turned to walk away, but she stopped when Daniel asked, "What? What did I do wrong?"

In response to the question, Rosie spun and faced Daniel. She had begun to cry.

"Just because I fucked you once don't make us a couple!" she blurted.

"But—" attempted Daniel, but Rosie cut him off.

"And I *know* you told Saul!"

Daniel's mouth snapped shut. *How?* He wondered.

"Because of you, he snuck into my bedroom window last night and raped me! He said you told him my momma worked nights! How could you Daniel? How could you?"

Rosie covered her face. Crying openly, she turned and ran back into the house, leaving Daniel where he was; standing beside the fence.

"I didn't know…" he mumbled sadly as he walked away.

#

5

Daniel always blamed his three divorces on the demands of his job, but he knew that wasn't the truth. He had grown cold and distant, and after seeing the evil people were capable of, it had become increasingly difficult for him to be intimate with women. Sure, he loved his wives and he believed they loved him too, but eventually…they *all* left. However, when he met Louise, Daniel had hoped things would be different, because she had a demanding job too. She was a struggling real estate agent.

On the day of their wedding, as he peered down into Louise's warm brown eyes, Daniel wondered, *Will she love me unconditionally? Have I finally found my true love?*

"I don't know!" he blurted, unintentionally, when the Magistrate asked if he took Louise to be his 'lawfully wedded wife'.

"I mean, yes…I do!" exclaimed Daniel, correcting himself, and the over worked civil servant smiled.

"Then you can kiss your bride," she said, closing her bible. The Magistrate stepped back, and after allowing Daniel and Louise a personal moment, she beckoned to the next couple; waiting in the foyer outside of her office to come in.

When the nervous groom saw the Magistrate, he leapt to his feet and was just about to lead his fiancé into the chamber, but the savvy bride grabbed his arm and held him back.

"Wait," she said, pointing toward Daniel and Louise. "Look!"

"Oh, okay…" responded the groom, and he sat back down.

#

Six months later, Daniel walked into his home, after a long day at the precinct, and Louise rushed to greet him from the kitchen. She was holding a beer in one hand and the T. V. remote in the other.

"Kiss me you fool!" she called to Daniel, and he wrapped his arms around Louise. Lifting her off the floor, Daniel spun around while kissing Louise.

"Mmmm, what was that for?" she asked, once Daniel had stopped and let her down.

Daniel grabbed the remote and beer, and without answering Louise's question, he walked to the sofa and sat. While drinking the beer, he pointed the remote at the television and it came on.

"That was good!" burped Daniel, after nearly drinking the entire bottle of beer.

"What, the beer?" inquired Louise when she walked over to the sofa and sat next to Daniel.

"—and the kiss too," he answered.

Thinking Louise wanted to cuddle; Daniel moved closer to her and looked into her face. Lovingly, he touched her face and thought, *where was this woman when I was a younger man? How could I have been so lucky?*

"What are you thinking about?" asked Louise. She suspected Daniel was thinking about work, and she wanted to get his mind off of it.

"Tell me it's something nice," she added with a kiss.

"Well, I was walking down the street today and saw a beautiful wildflower growing all by itself in the corner of this flower bed. It made me think of you, so I wrote you a poem."

"Really…? A poem…?"

Daniel had stopped romancing Louise, so she was surprised to hear he had written a poem.

"You *actually* wrote a poem?"

"What, you think I can't write poetry anymore? Don't think I got game?"

"No…it's just that," Louise stammered, unsure. She didn't want to sound unappreciative or hurt Daniel's fragile ego.

"It's just that…You know, after we got married you stopped doing…You know…the romantic stuff, like—"

"—Writing poetry? Yeah, I know and I'm sorry."

Daniel held up one finger and used it to silence Louise. He pressed it against her lips. Then he reached into his pocket and pulled out a crinkled sheet of paper.

"Okay, prepare to be *wooed*," he said, and cleared his throat.

"Wooed?"

"Yeah, wooed…Isn't that what I did to get you?"

"Yeah…you wooed me alright."

Daniel ignored Louise's sarcasm while un-crumpling the paper. He looked down at it, closed his eyes and swallowed noticeably. When he looked up again, Daniel saw the anticipation on Louise's face. He smiled, and closing his eyes once more, pressed the paper against his chest and said, "A butterfly brushed its wings against a slumbering flower…The clouds parted and sun light filled the sky. Believing it a sign, the butterfly became best friends with the flower, but it soon discovered the flower couldn't fly, so it flew off to find someone like itself."

Daniel paused. He took a moment and thought about the differences he and Louise had to overcome before marrying.

Louise was raised in a sheltered, well to do family. She was educated, beautiful, and outgoing; whereas Daniel was raised on the '*wrong*' side of the tracks. Something Louise's father pointed out. Daniel's life was a hard scrambled existence as he fought to rise above the gang violence and poverty he lived in and around.

"The wildflower refused to give up on true love, and did something unheard of in the plant world. It sprouted wings, and pursued the butterfly. The end…"

When Daniel opened his eyes, he saw Louise and she was crying.

"Com'on, it wasn't that bad. Was it?"

Louise rose from her seat. She rushed into Daniel's arms.

"No…it's not that," she said.

"Then what…what's the matter?"

"I don't know…I just I love you so much."

"I love you too, baby."

Daniel dropped the paper. He wrapped his arms around Louise, and they stood in the middle of the living room, holding each other.

"I feel foolish," Louise said when she released Daniel. She wiped her eyes, and feeling embarrassed, turned to go into the kitchen. "Sit down and watch the news, while I fix dinner."

Just as Louise walked away, she bent to pick up the balled up paper Daniel had dropped. But when he saw her do that, Daniel blurted, "Wait! I got that!"

Louise ignored Daniel and picked up the paper anyway. She looked back over her shoulder to Daniel, smiling.

"It's okay, sweetheart. I got it. Besides, I want to put it in my scrapbook. It was so sweet."

Daniel cringed, when Louise un-crinkled the paper and looked down at it.

"Daniel, I—I don't understand," mumbled Louise. She turned to face Daniel. "This is blank."

"I know…I know, please let me explain."

"Explain? What…that you made up that poem?"

"Baby please—" said Daniel, but Louise flung herself into his arms again.

#

6

    High rise condos, typically, are located in neighborhoods that the tenant's think are safe, and immune to crime. And why shouldn't they believe that? With all of the association fees they pay they expect top notch security; a Doorman controlling entry to the building and security cameras watching the premises, parking garage, and service entrances tirelessly.
    The condo that Daniel is standing in is one of the units that provided its owner a false sense of security, with its lavishly decorated and expensive living room. But Daniel knew how well the place was lain out, because he's been there before. He knows how comfortable the leather sofa dominating the living room is, because he's sat on it. The expensive paintings adorning the walls are familiar, because he purchased one or two of them as a house warming gift, several years back. Even the exotic sculptors lining the hallway are familiar, and they should be, because Daniel was present when some were picked out. He even helped move some into place, when they were delivered. Daniel remembers it all, because it's just as he last seen it, except for the bedroom. That was a mess. Clothes littered the floor and the drawers they had been in were out and lying haphazardly on the floor. The room appears as though someone was searching for something; jewelry or money. Lying across the lavishly adorned king size bed was the condo's occupant; nude and faced down, with her head dangling off one side.
    When Daniel walked into the bedroom, and over to the body, he dropped down to one knee in front of it, so he could look into her face. He needed to know it was her.

"Shit," he groaned when he saw Terrie's lifeless face.

#

Daniel had met Terrie one summer, thirty years ago, when she first visited her grandmother. He was sixteen and she was fourteen, and it was obvious they liked each other. But because Saul was the first on the block to meet her, he claimed the beautiful teenage debutant as his own. So, in accordance to the neighborhood's local rules, everyone left her alone and respected Saul's claim.

One day Daniel saw Terrie sitting alone at a picnic table in the park. Saul had gone to get them something to drink from Mr. Levi's convenience store. He walked up to her and introduced himself.

"So how long you and Saul been seeing each other?" he asked, and sat down at the table.

"We ain't *seeing* each other. Who told you that, Saul?"

Terrie was surprised by Daniel's question. She turned and looked toward the store. When she didn't see Saul, she turned back around and did something Daniel hadn't expected. She reached out and tried to touch his face, and then his hair.

"What are you doing?" Daniel pulled back and avoided Terrie's hand.

"Saul ain't my type," she answered, "I like 'em tall, and light skinned, like you…with all that curly hair."

"What about Saul?"

"What about him?"

"Well, he's sweet on you."

"I ain't trying to get with Saul. I got my eyes on you, and I always get what I want."

"Well, Saul and I are homeboys, and we don't steal each other's girls."

"I ain't his girl."

"That maybe, but he saw you first, and since he claimed you first, you're off limits to everyone, until he says different."

Terrie stood. Pouting, she turned and walked away.

"Well, we'll see 'bout that," she said.

"Hey, where are you going?"

"To tell Saul I already got a boyfriend."

"You do…who?"

"You…Silly!"

"No! Wait!"

Daniel leapt to his feet and rushed to catch Terrie.

"Don't do that!" he called out, so Terrie stopped and turned to face him.

"And why not?" she asked.

"Because he don't like being told no, if you know what I mean?" said Daniel, trying to explain. But when he saw Saul exiting the store, he stopped talking abruptly and returned to the picnic table.

After Daniel walked away, Terrie, suspecting he had seen Saul, looked back over her shoulder and there was Saul, crossing the street.

Throughout their conversation; Saul kept glancing pass Terrie toward Daniel. The anger he struggled to control was obvious, but when Terrie told him she wasn't his girl, he slammed the sodas down and stormed away.

After walking back to where Daniel was sitting, Terrie sat beside him. And they both sat silent for a moment. When she looked at Daniel, he shook his head.

"Well," sighed Terrie. "That could've gone better."

"You think?" asked Daniel as he stood to leave.

"Where are you going?" Terrie reached for Daniel, but he jerked his arm from her grasp.

"To find my friend, so I can tell him know I had nothing to do with this."

"But…I did this for us, so we could get together."

"Well, nobody asked you."

# # #

Many years later…

Terrie moved to Atlanta where she began her career as a nurse; working at the V.A. hospital. The first thing Terrie did when she got there was to call Daniel and invite him over.

"Wow! You've grown up," said Daniel, when he arrived at Terrie's condo, and saw her standing in her doorway.

Terrie screamed, "Danny!" and rushed into Daniel's arms.

Daniel stumbled back and nearly dropped the bottle of wine he had purchased as a house warming gift.

Terrie invited Daniel in. When she took his coat, she saw Daniel's badge and gun.

"You a cop?" she asked, while hanging up the coat.

"No…I'm a Detective." Daniel hated being called a cop.

"Then I guess I'd better hide my reefer, huh?"

"I only handle domestic homicides, not drugs, so it's all good."

"Really, who handles the drugs?"

"VICE does."

"Then it's okay if I burn a joint?"

"You got glaucoma?"

"No, I don't."

"Then I'd rather you didn't."

Daniel held up the wine.

"Sure, why not?" mumbled Terrie, disappointed. She had had a long day at the hospital and needed to wind down. When she headed toward the kitchen, to get the wine glasses, she suddenly remembering something and ran to her bedroom instead.

"Hey, I got something to show you!" she called out, while in the room. When Terrie returned, she was carrying an old picture album.

"What's that?" asked Daniel. He slid over to make room for Terrie on the sofa. When she sat, Daniel instantly recognized the perfume Terrie was wearing.

"You had it on the first day I met you, didn't you?"

Terrie nodded, impressed.

"You remember?"

Without answering, Daniel leaned closer to Terrie. Without asking permission, he reached around Terrie's head and pulled the pin holding her hair up, and her beautiful locks cascaded down pass her shoulders.

"I forgot about the hair," said Daniel. He reached up and ran his fingers through Terrie's silky black hair. He even held some up to his nose, so he could smell it.

"Ummm, you smell great!"

"Stop it, you're embarrassing me!" squealed Terrie, "and look at this!"

Terrie opened the book, so Daniel could see the black and white photos. They were pictures of people they both knew, back when they were teenagers. They laugh and giggle, when they saw the Afros and bellbottoms everyone wore, until they came upon a picture of Saul. In the picture he appeared angry and sullen, and he was standing all alone in the middle of a vacant lot.

"When's the last time you saw him?" asked Terrie. She looked up from the picture to Daniel.

"I don't know," answered Daniel, and while continuing to stare at the picture, he wondered, *what was he doing there, all alone?*

"Is he still alive?"

"I don't know," repeated Daniel. He looked up from the picture and into Terrie's sensuous eyes. Sitting back, Daniel shook his head and let out a sigh. *Jesus she's beautiful*, he thought, and then said, "We went our separate ways after you broke up with him. Our friendship was never the same after that. He thought I stole you from him."

"I'm sorry," replied Terrie, sounding regretful. She hadn't thought about that day, when she broke up with Saul, but now she remembered it clearly. Still, while looking into Daniel's eyes, she wanted to tell him how she truly felt about him.

"It's just that—" she began, but Daniel cut her off.

"Hey, don't sweat it! Besides, I heard through the grapevine, he moved out west and ended up in prison."

"Really…What did he do?"

"Shit, with Saul…ain't no telling," chuckled Daniel, and Terrie laughed. But when they stopped laughing an uncomfortable silence filled the room.

"Saul was into all kinds of stuff, by the time we graduated from high school."

Daniel was trying to fill the void. He looked down at the picture once more and continued talking.

"But you wouldn't know that would you, since you went back to Valdosta and never returned?"

"What are you talking about?" asked Terrie. She slapped the book close and leaned closer to Daniel. "I came back several times, but you had already moved on."

"Then how'd you get my number?"

"Well...I ran into one of your brother's at the *Greenbrier Mall*, when I first got here. He's the one that suggested I call you."

"LEAVE ME ALONE!" shouted Jeremy. He walked purposely across the parking lot, looking down at the ground and flailing his arms, as if he were trying to shoo something away. Jeremy, raised his feet, and high stepped, as though he were trying to prevent something from nipping at his heals.

"Dammit, leave me be!" he shouted again, and began to spin. It appeared as though he was chasing an imaginary tail. "If I get my hands on you, I'm gonna wring your neck!"

When Jeremy saw Terrie, he rushed up to her and began talking, as if he had been talking to her all along.

"Ain't seen you 'round these hea' parts in some time," he said and Terrie recoiled, when she turned her back to her car and faced him.

Jeremy was dirty and foul smelling. His hair had grown out long and it was hanging off his head in kinky bundles of dread locks. The beard on his face was nappy and littered with remnants of the moldy food he had scavenged from dumpsters behind fast food restaurants. His teeth were yellow and jagged, and several were missing.

Terrie quickly scanned the parking lot, hoping someone would come to her aid, but when no one did, she pulled her purse up close.

Flashing a weary smile, she reached inside it and pulled out a dollar bill. When she tried to give it to Jeremy, he refused it.

"I don't need your damn filthy money…whore, don't you know who I am?"

Terrie shook her head. Frightened, she tried to walk away, but Jeremy stepped in front of her and blocked her path. He moved in closer and forced Terrie to smell his reeking body, and foul breathe. When she raised her hand to her nose, Jeremy, not surprised by her reaction, looked down and said, "See, I told you. People can smell you."

"God," groaned Terrie.

"I'm sorry Terrie, but Roscoe's one foul fucker. I told 'em he needed a bath, but he says he don't need one."

Terrie pretended she understood what Jeremy was talking about, because she was curious as to how he knew her name.

"Do I know you?"

"You know my brother," replied Jeremy, but all of a sudden, he turned, and scrambling back a few feet, yelled, "Git now…git!"

When he returned, Jeremy was smiling, as if nothing had happened. But he cast a quick glance back over his shoulder, before looking at Terrie again.

"Damn thing won't leave me alone. Now, where was I?"

"You were just about to tell me who your brother is."

In response to Terrie, Jeremy reached into his pocket and pulled out a dirty crumbled up business card. He handed it to Terrie, and she looked down at it. When Terrie looked up again, she saw Jeremy had already walked away.

"Hey!" she called out, but Jeremy didn't stop walking. Instead, he just shouted, "Give 'em a call!"

# # #

"So…is that all?"

Daniel was dying to know more about his baby brother. It had been a long time since he had last seen or heard from him.

"Huh?"

"I mean, what else happened?"

"Well, after I realized who he was, I ran after Jeremy and invited him over. You know, so he could clean himself up; get something to eat. I was just trying to help. Anyway, after we got to my condo, and he cleaned himself up, we talked. He remembers everything; stuff I had forgotten about a long time ago."

"I'm just surprised he still had my number," said Daniel remembering the business card he had give Jeremy several years back. Because Jeremy had never called, Daniel figured he had thrown it away. *Good thing I hadn't changed that number*, he thought.

"You married?" Daniel asked Terrie, deciding to change the subject. Thinking about his paranoid homeless brother always bummed Daniel out.

"No," she answered, and then held out her hand, so Daniel could see she wore no ring. "You…?"

"No…not currently," answered Daniel.

"Now, what's that suppose to mean?"

"It means I've been married before, but I ain't now."

"Really, so how many times have you been married?"

Daniel held up both hands, and exaggerating, began to count multiple fingers.

"Six or seven…think," he joked, but when it became apparent Terrie had taken him seriously he said, "Hey, just kidding! Jesus…I can't believe you fell for that."

Terrie blushed and then playfully slapped Daniel's hands down.

"Well, you never know. After all, you were the *pretty boy* all the girls fawned over."

"I wasn't a pretty boy."

"Then tell me the truth, how many times have you been married…for real?"

"Three."

"Three? Really…?"

"Yeah and the last break up really hurt."

"I'm sorry to hear that," replied Terrie, and she stood. She walked away, and was about to go to her bedroom, but she stopped and looked back at Daniel curiously.

"You're not married now, are you?"

"No," he answered with a smile.

"Good!" responded Terrie, and she smiled too. Then she rushed into her bedroom and closed the door, but a moment later, re-opened it and stuck out her head.

"Hey, I ain't trying to be rude or anything, but I just got home from work and need to get out of this uniform. I'll be back in a moment, so make your self comfortable."

"It's cool, take your time."

Daniel got up and walked to the kitchen, where he searched for a glass.

"Hey, where are your wine glasses?" he asked, when he couldn't find one.

"They're in the cabinet…next to the fridge! The corkscrew's in the drawer next to the stove!"

"Wow…thin walls," mumbled Daniel, and Terrie, hearing him, answered, "Yeah, I know!"

Daniel looked up from the drawer he was about to open, and was surprised to hear Terrie's response. The first drawer contained eating utensil; spoons, forks and knives, but not a corkscrew. When Daniel opened the dishwasher, that's where he found the corkscrew, but it was dirty. He washed it, and then opened the bottle and poured himself a drink.

After strolling around the living room, admiring all of the art work, Daniel returned to the sofa and sat down. He sat his wine glass on the coaster on the coffee table and picked up the album again. He flipped quickly through the pages, until he saw a picture of himself wearing an Afro.

Daniel chuckled, and didn't know Terrie had slipped quietly out of her bedroom and was standing behind him. When she bent down, and looked over his shoulder to get a better look at the picture, Daniel reared back laughing so hard, he nearly bumped into her head.

"S'cuse me!" exclaimed Daniel. He stood, when he realized he wasn't alone, and turned to face Terrie. But when he saw what she was wearing, he nearly fell over backwards.

Terrie was wearing a Kimono robe, but it wasn't wrapped tightly around her body, as Japanese tradition dictates it should be. Instead, the beautifully adorned robe hung open and revealed everything Terrie's snug fitting nurse's uniform only implied.

"I—didn't—see—you—standing—there," stammered Daniel, while struggling not to stare at Terrie's beautiful nude body.

Terrie walked around the sofa and stood in front of Daniel. She reached out and ran her fingers through his curly hair, but this time Daniel didn't stop her.

"I always liked your hair," she cooed, and then let the robe drop unceremoniously to the floor.

Daniel, no longer bound by the unwritten rules of the old neighborhood, pulled Terrie close. His mouth found hers and they kissed.

Terrie's taste was intoxicating.

Daniel picked Terrie up and whisked her back to the bedroom, where he laid her on the bed. He kicked off his shoes and unbuttoned his trousers, but before he could lower them, they slipped from his grasp and dropped to the floor.

"Oh my!" gasped Terrie, when she saw Daniel's partially erect penis. "I had heard the rumors, when we were kids, but I never realized how big it *really* was."

Daniel bent and picked up his pants. He unclipped the cover to his handcuffs, and while facing Terrie, dangled them off one finger.

"So you're a freak, huh?" asked Terrie, smiling mischievously. "Hey, I got a little freak in me too. Just don't hurt me, okay?"

"Don't worry, I'll be gentle. You never know, you might like it."

The words Daniel spoke repeated, over and over in his head. He dropped the handcuffs, because the room began to spin. Stumbling backwards, Daniel bumped into a wall. His eyes rolled back in his head and everything went black. In the darkness, Daniel saw the little boy again, but this time, the boy was floating over Terrie's bed, flailing his arms frantically.

When Daniel opened his eyes again, he looked up at Terrie. However, instead of making love to him, she was reading a thermometer.

"Well, you don't have a fever," she said, and then placed one hand on Daniel's forehead. "How do you feel?"

"Okay...I guess," answered Daniel. He sat up. "What happened?"

"Nothing happened! That's what happened...nothing at all!" exclaimed Terrie. She stood and stepped back, and then, with a side to side motion, she shook her breast.

"I guess, when you saw the *sisters*, you couldn't handle the possibilities and passed out."

"Sorry," replied Daniel, sheepishly. He pulled himself up off the floor and walked over to the bed, where he sat down. "I don't know what came over me. Tired, I guess."

"You whimpered like a baby. Is everything all right?" asked Terrie, while she walked over to a table that had a pitcher of water on it. She poured out a glass of the water, and then after sitting the pitcher down, picked up a small brown bottle. She opened it and shook out two small white pills.

"I hear cries like that all the time at the V.A," she said, with a backward glance at Daniel. "Old soldiers fighting a war, in their dreams, that's been over for decades."

When Terrie returned to the bed, she held out the pills and the water.

"Here, these will help you sleep."

"What are they?"

"Don't worry, they're harmless."

"I don't think so."

"Why not, you need them?"

"Because...I have to answer my phone, if I get a call during the night."

"Does your job always call you at night, after you've gone to bed?"

"Unfortunately, yes...It comes with the territory."

Terrie popped the pills into her own mouth and walked back to the table. She drank the water and sat the empty glass on the table.

"Look, you're welcome to spend the night," she said when she turned to face Daniel. "But don't try any hanky-panky while I'm sleeping. You had your chance."

"Don't worry," replied Daniel, with a wry smiled. "I'm the police…You're safe with me."

# # #

7

Daniel turned away from Terrie's mutilated body. He looked over at Becky. She was standing next to the table on the far side of the room, staring down at something.

"Take a look at this, will you?"

She was pointing at the yellow note pad lying next to the water pitcher.

Daniel stood and hurrying, crossed the room in three long strides.

"No…No…No," he said, shaking his head profusely. "This ain't a suicide."

"Who said anything about suicide, unless you know something about this victim too? Do you know her? Was she suicidal?"

Daniel didn't offer up any answers. Instead, he reached into his pocket and pulled out a pair of latex gloves. Using them incorrectly, he folded the gloves over the edge of the note pad and picked it up. He began to read out loud.

"Born to die…Born in fifty-nine…Told I would die before my time…Put to work at ten…Told Santa was dead at twelve…Now tell me, ain't I livin' in hell?"

Daniel paused and looked up at Becky. She shrugged, so Daniel continued.

"My life's one great big fuck up…No good fortune, no good luck…Born in fifty-nine…Told I would die before my time…"

"Shesh," sighed Daniel. He dropped the pad and turned away from the table. He looked back at Becky.

"Anything else?" he asked.

"Naw," answered Becky with a slight nod of her head. She turned to face the bed. "But I think our Vic was raped, looks like she put up a good fight too. "

"What brings you to that conclusion?"

"Because there's flesh under her nails, and I found a used rubber in the bathroom trash too. There's still some fluid in its reservoir, so I'm gonna take it back to the lab and see if I can pull a DNA sample from it. If I can, I'll run it against known cons."

Daniel walked back over to the bed. He knelt next to it, so he could get a better look at Terrie's wounds, but when he leaned in closer to it, the scent of her perfume suddenly overwhelmed him. Startled by it, he stood and stepped back.

"Whoa!" he exclaimed, fighting back the rush of memories the scent had awakened.

"What?" said Becky, and she rushed to where Daniel was standing. "Did you see something?"

When Daniel didn't answer Becky knelt and took a closer look at Terrie's face.

"Look at her expression," she said, looking back over her shoulder to Daniel. "She was surprised when this happened."

"How do you figure that?"

"Look at her eyes. Can't you see she was terrified?"

Daniel stepped closer and fighting pass the smell, stared clinically down into Terrie's eyes, hoping to see what Becky saw. When he couldn't, he turned away and fixated his eyes on the open bay window.

"Make sure you dust that too," he said, disregarding the fact the condo was several floors off the ground.

Becky walked over to the window with her print kit. Just as she began to examine it for prints, she spotted the coroner. She was late, because Daniel had made her wait too, just as he had done to her.

"You can take her now," Daniel said when he saw the angry coroner. He stepped aside, and granted her access to Terrie's body.

When Daniel saw Becky packing up her print kit he said, "Anything?"

"No…nothing," she sighed and was about to say something else, when Daniel turned and walked away.

"Okay. Let me know when you find something."

"Sure thing," replied Becky. She walked to the other side of the room and began processing the water pitcher and note pad for prints.

"This guy is smart," said Daniel, talking to . "But if he thinks I'm gonna give up he's got another think coming."

"Who said anything 'bout giving up?"

Daniel looked around to find Becky down on her knees, spraying luminal on the carpet.

"Hey! Take a look at this!" she exclaimed, pointing beneath the bed.

"What is it?"

"Get down here, and take a look!"

Becky held up the bloody bed sheet, and Daniel, dropping down on one knee, looked under the bed. He saw a rose.

"Son-of-a-bitch!" he groaned, "That flower connects this murder to the Congress Center murders."

Daniel reached beneath the bed and grabbed the rose. Holding it up, he looked at Becky and said, "Make sure none of your guys say anything to the press. I can just see it now, 'ROSE KILLER STRIKES AGAIN!'"

"Don't worry," replied Becky, but before she could say anything more, a news crew burst into the room with cameras rolling.

"Detective Rose!" shouts the reporter, "any comments? Is this related, in any way, to the murders behind the Congress Center?"

Daniel stood and stepped in front of Terrie's body. Then he rushed forward and pushed the reporter and her cameraman backwards, toward the door. Once they were all outside the condo he said, "Look, what happened behind the Congress Center has absolutely nothing to do with this crime; pure and simple."

"Was this victim's throat slashed too? Was she raped?"

"Look, god dammit! These crimes are not connected…period!"

# # #

8

Louise reached for Daniel in the darkness, but he wasn't there. When she raised her head and looked back, she saw his side of the bed was empty.

"Daniel," she called out softly.

When Louise looked around, she discovered Daniel standing in front of their bedroom window. He was staring out into the dark sky.

Louise pulls back her covers, gets out of bed, and walks over to Daniel. With him facing the window, she wraps her arms around his back and lays her head against his back. She feels him trembling.

"Bad dream?"

Daniel nods. "Uh-huh," he answers. It sounds as though he has been crying.

"Was it the little boy again?"

"Yeah…"

"Wanna talk about it?"

"No!" blurts Daniel, but realizing how he must've sound, he snapped his mouth shut, and shakes his head. Turning, Daniel wrapped his arms around Louise and squeezes her.

When Louise looked up, and into Daniel's sad face, she saw a tear moved slowly down his cheek.

"Honey, I'm worried. It's not normal to keep having the same dream, over and over again."

"I'm alright," insists Daniel.

"But—"

"It'll be okay!" snaps Daniel. He releases Louise and turns toward the window once more.

"But, baby…" attempts Louise, but Daniel, still reeling emotionally from the dream, barks, "I don't want to talk about it!"

"I'm sorry," Louise replies. She attempted to touch Daniel's shoulder, but he pulled away.

"Don't—" he says, walking away.

"Daniel…honey, I'm here for you."

Daniel stopped and glanced back at Louise.

"I know," he replied with a warm smile, and trying to sound upbeat, adds, "Look, I've got paperwork to catch up on, so why don't you go on back to bed. I'll be downstairs in the study finishing up; should've done it a long time ago. And don't worry, it won't take long. I'll be back to bed before you know it…Okay?"

Louise doesn't respond, and instead, walks to her closet. She pulled out a robe and put it on. Then she walked pass Daniel, out of the bedroom, and toward the kitchen.

"Okay…I'll fix you some breakfast and coffee."

"Honey, no, I—"

Louise stopped abruptly and spun around to face Daniel. There was a stern look on her face.

"Daniel…You're just going to go down stairs, work for a while, and then think of an excuse to go to your office; where you feel safer. So let's not play games with each other, okay? It's too damn late for that crap."

"Okay, but…"

Louise knew Daniel well, because that's exactly what he had planned on doing.

#

9

It's the middle of the night and the squad room's empty. All of the uniformed officers are out on patrol, and so are the night shift detectives; investigating calls. The only person present is watch commander, Captain Darryl Peterson.

The captain, a career law enforcement officer, is a true professional. He is a straight shooter who won't hesitate to call a spade a spade. He means what he says, and says what he means. Everyone trusts and respects him, which is how he ended up on the fast track to becoming the Chief of Police. However, somewhere along the way, his star stopped rising. Because ten years earlier, Darryl's morals and ethics were put to the test, when a young hooker was severely beaten, and nearly killed, by the city's mayor.

Darryl was head of the Mayor's personal security detail, and he was also the prosecutor's number one witness. The call he received that night still haunts him.

"Darryl, me boy…"

It was Mayor Tim Kelso, his voice was agitated, but Darryl instantly recognizes his thick Irish accent. The mayor was a Chicago native, born and bred, and although he led the south's largest city, his political style was unmistakably Chicagoan; rough and tough. Tim had paid his dues, and having managed to survive the politics of the dirty south, earned the respect of the southern movers and shakers.

"Tim…everything okay?"

Darryl was at home relaxing, watching a rented movie, when he got the call.

"Hell naw!"

The mayor was drunk. His voice was slurred and he blended his words into a unique southern-Irish twang.

"What's wrong?" asked Darryl, knowing the only reason Tim would call directly was only because something was amiss.

"I done fucked up."

"What did you do? Where are you?"

Darryl picked up his remote and pressed the mute button, silencing the television.

"Can't talk about it over the phone," answered Tim. Feeling paranoid, he lowers his voice. "Someone might be listening in."

"Are you hurt?" asks Darryl, concerned, but at the same time, annoyed by the call.

"Naw, I ain't hurt."

"Then tell me where you are," said Darryl, but then he hears the sound of a drawer opening and closing, with a loud bang.

Tim, searching for something with an address on it, finds an ashtray and a book of matches. The ashtray was clear, but the match book has the hotel's logo printed on the outside. Tim flips over the matches, looking for an address, but sees nothing. He opens it and sees the hotel's address, imprinted on the inside.

"Uh, I'm at the Towers…Baker and Harris…room 1113."

"Good, stay put!"

Darryl points the remote at the television once more, but this time he pressed the off button and the picture goes black.

"Do you need medical care?" he asked, standing.

"Naw…I—"

A loud crashing sound reverberated in Daryl's ear, because Tim dropped the phone. Someone screams, and then Darryl hears Tim cuss and yell; telling the screaming person to shut up.

"You still there?" asked Tim, after he picked up the phone again.

"What the hell's going on Tim, and where the hell is your security detachment?"

"They outside, but I don't want them in here. Got'ta keep this on the down low...you get my drift?"

Darryl knew Tim well, and understood what he meant.

"I'll be there in ten," he replied. "Just hold tight. You hear me—"

The phone went dead, so Darryl angrily flips his cell shut and rushes toward the door.

#

At the Towers Hotel, Darryl gets out of his cruiser and hands the keys to the man holding open his door. The Doorman knows why Darryl is there, and he says, "Mayor's been running whores in and out of here all evening, Captain."

The Doorman closed the door and rushed ahead of Darryl, so he could open the door.

"Wife must've cut him off again," he chuckles.

When Darryl heard the flippant comment, he glared at the doorman, but he knew how the business worked. So, reaching into his inside coat pocket for his wallet, Darryl retrieves a crisp one hundred-dollar bill and stuffs it into the Doorman's hand.

"This goes nowhere and if I hear about it on the tube tomorrow, or read about it in the papers, I'll know who the source is. Understand?"

"Uh, not a word," the doorman gulped.

#

The Towers Hotel is upscale and very expensive. The only people that typically can afford to stay there are entertainers, actors, professional sports athletes, and politicians. The staff; well trained and professionals in their own right, are accustomed to seeing famous people. They know to look the other way, when necessary, and to keep their mouth's shut. So when they saw the string of hookers coming, and going to the penthouse, they looked the other way. Even when they heard screams, and cries for help, no one thought to call the police, particularly since there were two of them standing outside the mayor's room. The way they figured it, if the mayor *really* needed help, they would help.

When Darryl exited the elevator, he immediately heard screaming. He rushed down the hall and found his two subordinate officers standing casually outside the room. One was talking on a cell phone, while the other read a magazine.

"What the hell's going on here?"

When the officer on the cell phone heard Darryl, he turned his back to him, not realizing just who he was. However, when the other officer reading the magazine looked up, he dropped the magazine and snapped to attention.

"God dammit, I'm talking to you!"

Darryl rushed pass the officer standing at attention and to the one on the phone. He snatched it out of the derelict officer's hand, and slammed it against the floor.

"Hey—" protested the officer, but when he saw Darryl, he shut his mouth, and stood erect.

Darryl shoved the officer aside, but when he reached for the doorknob and it didn't open, stepped back and looked at the officer nearest the door.

"Key…?"

"We don't have it," replied the officer, so Darryl threw his shoulder against the door and it came off its hinges.

Inside the room, lying on the bed, and covered with a blood soaked sheet, was a teenage hooker.

"Are you okay?" asks Darryl, and her rushes to her aid. "Miss, are you okay?"

When the girl doesn't a voice speaks from the bathroom.

"Aye Lad'de, I'm alright."

Darryl turned and spots the mayor. He's standing in front of the bathroom mirror, staring at the scratches on his face.

"Bleeden' bitch scratched me face though," he says, glances back over his shoulder toward Daniel. "Don't know how I'm gonna explain this to the wife though."

"This girl needs medical attention," said Darryl, while looking down at the girl.

"Fuck that bitch, and just do me a favor, will you? Make sure she disappears, okay?"

"Tim…" Darryl shook his head. "This shit has got to stop!"

"What are you talking 'bout?" asks Tim innocently, pretending not to know what Darryl meant. He turned around and faces Darryl.

"THIS TIM, THIS!" barked Darryl. He stands and asked, "And what did this one do this time?"

This wasn't the first time Tim had beaten a hooker, and it wasn't the first time he had asked Darryl to clean up his mess.

Tim smirked, and he walks out of the bathroom and begins to dress.

"Buggerin' bitch thought she was too good to get butt-fucked. Said she was an anal virgin…" Tim spat on the girl's face. "Fuck'n whore ain't a virgin, not anymore she ain't."

When Tim realized the door was open, and that his security detail, along with a housekeeper, is staring at him, listening to everything being said; he rushed forward and slams it shut, but the door wouldn't stay closed.

"God dam'mit!" he barked angrily, while pressing his back against the closed door. Glaring angrily at Darryl he says, "Now everyone's gonna hear about this! Fuck all!"

Darryl doesn't react to Tim's angry outburst. Instead, he reached into his pocket for his cell phone.

"What'cha think you're doing?" asked Tim, curiously, when he saw the phone.

"I'm calling for a bus. This girl needs medical attention. She's unconscious."

"Unconscious—"

Tim rushed over to the bed, and slapped the hooker, until she lets out a mournful whimper.

"See," he said, relieved, "She's just sleeping."

"No, she ain't!"

Darryl pushed Tim aside, so he could check the girl's pulse. It's shallow. Her heart's still beating

"See, like I told you, she's just sleeping. Hell, I out'ta know," said Tim, chuckling. "Cause I rocked that bleeden bitch's world."

Darryl was angry, because of Tim's cold and uncaring attitude, so he slapped him with the back of his hand. Then he grabbed Tim by the back of his neck and slammed him to the floor. With one knee in the small of Tim's back, Darryl grabs his arms and pulls them behind his back. He slaps handcuffs on one wrist, and then the other.

"God dam'mit Tim, you nearly killed her!" barked Darryl as he pulls Tim up to his feet.

"Darryl," Tim says, calmly and calculating. "You need to consider well what it is you're doin'?"

"I have, and sir…you're under arrest."

Darryl looked back at the bewildered officers that are still standing in the hallway watching. He signaled for them to come into the room.

"Take him to the station, and be sure to use the back entrance."

The officers rushed forward, and grabbed Tim by his cuffed arms. Just as they are about to exit the room, Darryl reminds them of the trouble they were in.

"I want both of you in my office first thing in the morning, so we can discuss your futures. Do I make myself clear?"

"Yes sir!" reply the officers, speaking in unison.

"You've just buggered your career, Peterson! You know that?" shouts Tim as he's led away.

"Yeah…" mumbled Darryl. "I know."

#

Juries hate politicians that abuse the public's trust, particularly those who commit violent crimes while in office. So when Mayor Tim Kelso heard Darryl testify, he knew his fate was sealed.

"Ladies and gentlemen of the jury, what say you?" asks the Judge, and the foreperson, a middle aged woman, stood.

"Your honor, on the first count of *rape in the first degree*, we find the defendant guilty."

A low murmur of whispers traveled from one side of the court room to the other. The judge pounded his gavel, and barked, "Order...order in the court!"

Once the noise abates, the foreperson says, "Regarding the second count of *aggravated assault in the first degree*, we find the defendant guilty."

Several reporters rush from the courtroom with cell phones in hand. The judge pounds his gavel once more. When he looks at the defense table, he discovers Tim had sat back down.

"Mister Kelso, stand up!"

"Huh?" said Tim, and he looked up. He had been staring down at the table, contemplating his fate, and had not put much thought into what he had done, when he sat down. So when the judge shouted for the Bailiff to go over and force him to stand, Tim held up his hands and stood.

"Okay...Okay," he said, "No call to go and get all physical."

"Sir, you are a disgrace—" began the judge. His voice was loud and didn't really require the microphone mounted to his desk.

"—A sitting Mayor...do you have anything to say before I render sentence?"

"Please, just send me to a federal facility and not a state prison."

Tim's lawyer raises a hand to his mouth, and cleared his throat loudly. Tim, understanding he hadn't shown any respect, when he asked to be sent to a federal prison, added, "Your honor..."

The judge glared at Tim for a long time, before responding. When he finally looked down at his file, he let out an audible sigh of frustration. He signed off on the jury's verdict, and then said, "Having been found guilty, by a jury of your peers, I sentence you to five years on the first count, and five years on the second. Both sentences are to run concurrently. You are to be taken immediately from this courthouse, and placed into the custody of the Federal bureau of prisons, where you're to be transported to a facility of their choosing. Good luck and good riddance!"

The judge raised his gavel and slammed it down twice, before gesturing for the Bailiff to take Tim away.

###

The bus doors opened and Tim, along with forty other convicts, is ushered into the intake unit of the Taft Federal Prison. There he is given a physical, clothing, and bedding. His picture is taken again, and he's assigned a number. After all of that, Tim is escorted to a pod where he is assigned a cell; B125.

"Step inside and back away from the door" orders the guard, and Tim, doing as he's told; steps inside the cell and moves away from the open door.

After the door slides shut, Tim hears grunting and groaning, so he turns around and sees a large black man sitting on the commode, in the back of the cell. Dropping his meager belongings, Tim clinches his fist.

"What do you want to do, fuck or fight?"

The black man's lips slowly part, forming a menacing grin on his face. He looks like a wolf that's just cornered its prey. He stands, and with his pants still down around his ankles, steps forward.

"Depends on you," he answers. "I like fucking, but you ain't my type, so we can fight though, if that's what it's going to take to insure I get a good night's sleep; without being shanked."

Tim sighed. Relieved, he smiles, because he didn't like the idea of being corn holed. And he didn't want to fight either, because he knew he didn't have an ice cube's chance in hell against his cellmate. So being the old politician he was, he decided the best thing to do was make him his friend, and he holds out his hand.

"Me names Timothy, but me friends call me Tim."

The large black man, still standing with his pants down, quickly assessed Tim, and after determining he didn't pose a threat, extended his oversized hand.

"Mah name's Solomon, but most folk call me Saul."

"Then Saul it is, me boy!"

When Saul released Tim's hand, Tim picked up his things and looked at both bunks.

"Which one's mine?"

Saul placed one hand on the top bunk and said, "This one." Then he backed up and returned to the commode, where he finished his shit.

#

10

"Rose!"

Captain Peterson's baritone voice echoed throughout the empty squad room. He had not expected to see Daniel, until morning.

"What the hell are you doing here this time of the night? Somebody call you in?"

"Naw."

Daniel walked toward his desk, with his head down, trying to ignore the curious captain.

"Then what are you doing here, because if it ain't got anything to do with the cases I've assigned you, then you ain't getting paid over-time for being here so early."

Daniel dropped his briefcase on his desk and opens it. He pulled out his laptop and a manila folder.

"This is on my own dime cap," he responds, but when he looks up, the captain had gone back into his office. But a moment later, he re-emerges.

"Rose, I need to talk to you…bring your narrow ass in here."

"Shit," groaned Daniel. He had left his house, because he didn't want to talk to his wife, and now here he was, forced to talk to her father.

Daniel closed the folder, and was about to drop it back into his briefcase when the captain said, "And bring that with you too!"

#

After stepping into the captain's office, Daniel stood quietly in front of his desk; waiting to be offered a seat, but the offer never came.

"You got anything more on those two cases you caught this past week?" asked the captain, looking up from his seat. He leaned forward, and reached for the folder Daniel held.

"No, the M.O.'s appear similar, but I don't think the cases are related."

"Really...?"

Captain Peterson stared at the crime scene photos, searching for a clue. He looked like a hound dog searching for a scent. And even though he had seen many crime scene photos in his career, these turned his stomach.

"All of their throats were slashed, weren't they?" he commented and looked up at Daniel.

When Daniel shrugged, the captain continued with his unsolicited opinion.

"The wounds look similar too...could have been made by the same type of weapon."

"Yeah, maybe..."

Daniel, deciding the captain wasn't going to offer him a seat, sat down, but when he did that, the Captain Peterson looked up from the pictures disapprovingly. But, since no one else was around, he decided not to say anything.

"What do you mean, 'maybe'?" he asked, and held up one picture. "Have you even looked at these?"

Frustrated with his son-in-law, the captain tossed the gruesome photos onto his desk, so they both could see them. And then he points at them.

"You think it's just a coincidence? And what's the deal with these flowers?"

"Roses," said Daniel, correcting the captain.

"Huh...?"

The captain glanced down at the picture again, and Daniel said, "They're roses," which prompts the captain to bellow, "I don't give a fuck what they are!"

"Captain, the Vic's got nothing in common."

Daniel stands and begins to stuff the pictures back into the folder.

"Sure…two were prostitutes, but the third was a career nurse. She worked at the V.A. hospital."

"Yeah, well…" the rough edges on the captain's voice softened, "You better check out her background, because…as I understand it, that apartment was way beyond the pay scale of a nurse. She may have been moonlighting as a call girl."

"Sir, I don't think so, because I—"

Daniel stopped talking abruptly, short of revealing his past relationship with Terrie.

"Look, I don't believe in coincidences, so check it out anyway."

"Okay cap," replies Daniel, and then he turned to leave.

"I mean it," emphasized the captain, "a good detective leaves no stone unturned."

The captain pushed back from his desk, and opened its top drawer. He grabbed the folded newspaper, that's inside the drawer, and tossed it on the desk.

"Here!"

"What's that?" asked Daniel. He looked down at the paper.

"It's the early edition of today's paper. I got a buddy who works for the Journal. He gives me the front page, from time to time, before it hits the street. In case I got any comments."

"Well fuck me!" exclaimed Daniel, when he saw his picture on the front page.

Daniel was standing next to Becky in the picture, and he was holding the rose they discovered beneath Terrie's bed. Behind them, superimposed in the background, lies Terrie's mutilated body. And printed in bold letters, beneath the picture, is **"ROSE KILLER STRIKES AGAIN!"**

"What do you know about that?" asked the captain. "You know the department's policy regarding the press, and unauthorized comments, don't you?"

"Of course I do," retorts Daniel, angrily.

"Then where'd this come from?"

"I don't know, but I sure as hell gonna find out."

Daniel turned, and was about to exit the office again, but Captain Peterson stopped him.

"Hey, I ain't finish with you yet!" he barked, and Daniel spun around on his heels.

"What…What else do you want, I got work to do?"

"Hey, check that tone!"

"Sorry cap," replied Daniel, in deference, but when the captain smiles, he relaxes.

"So how's my daughter doing? You treating her right ain't 'cha?"

"Yeah, cap. She's an angel. I'm lucky to have her."

"Damn right you are!"

Darryl walked around his desk, and places an arm around Daniel's shoulders. He walks him out of his office.

"You know, you can talk to me…if you two are having problems."

"I appreciate that cap, but we'll be okay."

"Uh-huh…She says you keep having nightmares about some little boy. Son, you can't save 'em all. You got to let that shit go."

Daniel pursed his lips tightly, because he was upset Louise had confided in her father. But he knew Captain Peterson was right. Still, he knew the little boy in his dreams wasn't one from the cases he's investigated. He was someone else, someone closer. He just couldn't put a finger on the face he saw in the dreams.

'Cap, I got this…Okay?"

Captain Peterson stared into Daniel's tired eyes for a moment and remembered how energetic they were, when he first joined his unit. He knew the detective was smart and focused, otherwise he would have never allowed him to marry his daughter

"Okay…now take your ass out there, and solve those *'Rose'* murders, before this all blows up in our faces."

# # #

Back at his desk, Daniel pulled out the crime scene pictures again. When he looked at Rosemary's picture he imagined she was sleeping, but when he looked at Cecilia's, Daniel saw the anguish on her face. It was contorted grotesquely as if she were still experiencing the pain of her murder.

I don't believe in coincidences either, he thought. *This has got to be someone who knows me, but who?*

Frustrated, Daniel shakes his head and squeezes his temples, trying to force himself to remember the one person from his past that was twisted enough to go after the women he's known, instead of coming after him.

Did one of the boys get out of prison early? Daniel wonders and decides to check the Department of Correction's data base of recent releases. He turns on his laptop, and while waiting for it to power up, unlocks the file drawer where he keeps his hardcopy files. There are a number of old case files to choose from, but Daniel picks one that contains only a single sheet of paper. It has a list of names on it and written next to each name is the crime that person committed, and the amount of time he received. Several of the names had a red line drawn through them, and the word *dead* scribbled, in Daniel's handwriting, above the names. When nothing on the paper leaps out at Daniel, he glances at his laptop to see its waiting for him to enter a password. So he types in Louise's middle name and waits some more. After the department's antiquated intranet server connects, Daniel types his case's particulars into the profile template, and waits some more.

"Well, I'll be damned!" he exclaimed, when he saw what the computer kicked out. There were two more murders matching the profile Daniel had input.

The '*ding*' of the elevator sounded and Daniel looked, after he heard voices; people talking and laughing. The day shift is starting and the people getting off the elevator are filled with energy and ready to go to work. Most of them are the career nine to fivers, except for the detective wearing the baggy pants and oversized wife beater. It looks as though the detective was just released from some holding cell, because his hair is ruffled and his eyes are red, from the lack of sleep. But Daniel knows different. He knows the detective is a dedicated undercover detective, and that he never steps out of character. His name is Robney, and he and Daniel were friends. At least they used to be, until after they graduated from the academy and Daniel earned his detective's badge first. Robney resented Daniel, and he wasn't shy about expressing his feelings either.

"Still trying to impress the captain?" asked Robney, when he walked into the squad room and saw Daniel sitting at his desk. "Hell, he already lets you fuck his daughter. What more do you want?"

"That's my wife you're talking about."

"Oh yeah…your wife," replied Robney, with a suggestive flick of his tongue.

"Fuck off Rob, and grow up, will you?"

Daniel shut off his laptop and packing it up, tried to ignore Robney.

"Grow up…really?"

When Daniel looked up from his laptop, Robney gestures toward the men's room with a tilt of his head.

"Why don't you step into my office, so I can show you just how much I've grown?"

Robney grabbed his crotch with one hand, and while giving it a shake, points toward the toilet with his other.

Daniel stands. Accepting the challenge, he kicked his chair back. It flew across the room and slammed, loudly, into another desk.

"Yeah, that's it pretty boy…come and get some."

With fist clinched, Daniel steps forward, but Robney backs away. He wants Daniel to follow him into the restroom.

"I've wanted to kick your ass for some time now, and when I'm through, I'm going after that pretty little filly you've got stalled," he says, taunting Daniel.

When Captain Peterson heard the commotion in the squad room, he got up and looked out of his office. He sees Daniel and Robney squaring off.

"Hey! What the hell's gotten into you two? Rose! Ain't you got something needing to be done?"

"Yeah, but—" attempts Daniel. Lowering his clinched fist, he looks toward the captain.

"Don't but me. You got a major fucking crime to investigate, so get going!"

"Yeah…Detective," interjects Robney. "Get 'yo ass out there, like a *good* field nigger!"

When Captain Peterson hears Robney's comment, he focuses on him, and shouts, "Morris, bring your stupid ass here!"

Because Robney hesitated, the captain points toward the spot on the floor directly in front of him.

"Now goddam it, now!" he barked, but before walking away, Robney looks back at Daniel.

"You fucker," he growls, because he knows he's in trouble…again.

"Yeah, well…fuck you too!"

Daniel's voice echoes and everyone in the squad room hears him. He returns to his desk and finishes packing up his laptop, and files. After that, Daniel stormed out of the squad room and to the hallway, where he waited, angrily, for the elevator.

# # #

11

Daniel didn't like the morgue, but that never prevented him from visiting it in search of answers.

After walking through the double doors leading down to the morgue, a chill moved down Daniel's spine when he came to a hallway filled with gurneys; each contained a body. *Even in death we have to wait our turn*, though Daniel as he rushed passed the macabre scene.

Pushing open a second set of double doors, Daniel came upon several masked men hovering ghoulishly over four separate autopsy tables. Each of them was covered in blood, while splayed open on the tables, like butchered animals, were the remains of the recently deceased.

Daniel's throat spasm, and while looking for a trash can, he covered his mouth with his hand. When he saw a small waste basket sitting next to a desk, Daniel rushed to it and barfed.

"See boys…what happens when you drop in on a girl unannounced?" said a soft oriental voice from the far end of the room. The voice belong to the city's diminutive coroner, Vannie Tran

Vannie had been standing, on a small step ladder, next to one of her assistants when Daniel came into the room. After witnessing him puke, she hopped off the ladder and rushed over to a sink, where she pulled a paper towel out of the dispenser on the wall. She walked over to Daniel and handed him the towel.

"You should be used to this by now, Detective."

Daniel glanced up from the waste basket, and without acknowledging Vannie, took the towel.

"You'd think so," he answered after wiping his mouth.

When Daniel stood, he looked around and saw none of the assistants had stopped their ghoulish work.

"Got anything yet?" he asked, turning away from the ghouls to look down at Vannie.

"Well…the victims were sliced open by a sharp knife," answered Vannie, but then she emphasized, "A *very* sharp knife. Other than that, no…I don't have anything else for you."

Daniel sighed. His frustration was evident and showed on his face.

"Is there something else on your mind, Detective?" ask Van, while staring curiously up at Daniel's haggard face.

"Yeah, I need to know if these two murders are related."

Van walked to her cluttered desk, but before doing anything there, she glanced longingly at a picture taped to the side of her computer monitor. It was one she had taken while on last vacation.

After pushing aside several files, Vannie picked up one, but seeing it wasn't the one she was seeking, she tosses it carelessly aside. She picks up another group of files and flipped through them, until she finds the one she is searching for. With the file open, Vannie read her findings, and then let out a soft, mournful, sigh.

"Yeah, the cases are in my professional opinion, related. And I think the doer knows we're searching for him too, because he's being careful not to leave any trace evidence behind; no semen; no hair follicles, saliva…no nothing."

"So what makes them related?"

Daniel reached into his pocket and pulled out his note pad. He opened it, and flipped passed several full pages, until he found a blank one. He scribbled down the date and time. Below that, he writes 'Coroner.'

"The first two were hookers," said Daniel, when he looked up. "So I didn't expect any viable semen samples from them, but it seemed obvious the last Vic—"

Daniel paused abruptly, and swallowed down the word *'victim'*. He didn't like referring to Terrie in that manner.

"Uh...the last girl was raped."

"You're right in one aspect," answered Vannie, "She had sex, but I think it was consensual."

"What makes you think that?"

"Because...," continued Vannie, still reading her notes. "There weren't any vaginal tears, or bruising, and I didn't find any particulates under her fingernails. Adding all of that together, it leads me to believe she had consensual sex first, and then killed sometime later. If I had to guess, I'd say she was probably sleeping it off; from a wild night of fucking—"

Vannie glanced up from the file, and was about to smile at the thought of a wild night of sex, but decides against doing that, because Daniel didn't seemed to be amused by her flippant comment.

"Uh...what I meant to say is, I think the killer crept up to her and grabbed her by the hair."

The diminutive doctor clinched her small fist, and pretending she was grabbing hold of someone's hair, yanked her arm back violently.

"He yanked like this, and all in one motion, slit her throat before she knew what was happening."

"What about the semen samples taken at the scene? Who do they belong to?"

"Good question!" Vannie held one finger in the air. "I ran the sample against our national DNA data base, and got a hit."

"Fantastic!" Daniel was excited to have finally gotten a break. "Got a name?"

"She had sex with an ex-con named Solomon Thompson."

Vannie, still reading from her notes, looked up and saw a quizzical look on Daniel's face.

"Saul...Thompson? Saul Thompson?"

"Yeah...you know him?" asked Vannie, but before Daniel could answer she said, "Well, that don't matter, because his M.O. is strictly B & E, not sex crimes; particularly, the type that end up as a homicide. Besides, he's been locked up for quite awhile now."

"Yeah, well…I've got to check up on that."

Daniel wrote Saul's name in his note pad. He closed it and looked up, curiously around the room.

"I understand you have other homicides similar to mine."

"Sure do, you catch those too?"

"Naw…just was checking every lead. How many you got?"

Vannie holds up two fingers. She drops the file she holding, and picks up another one. Moving away from her desk, she walks over to a large bank of metal drawers and stops in front of one. After comparing the file's ID number against the ID number listed on the drawer, Vannie pulls open the drawer.

Daniel immediately recognizes Annette Sanchez.

# # #

12

Sandra and her father argued constantly, after he found out she had been sneaking Saul into her bedroom. He was a traditionalist, and even thought it was apparent to him his daughter was no longer a virgin; he refused to allow her to continue seeing Saul. But Sandra, for some odd reason, thought Saul was her soul mate. So when her father left for work that particular day, she snuck out and went across the street to Annette's house. She convinced Annette to run away with her, despite her age. The girls were friends, and friends stick together. Besides, being only thirteen herself, Sandra was afraid to run away alone.

The first place the two runaway's visited was the '*Little Park*' where Saul played basketball with his friends. When they got there, Sandra rushed to the edge of the court so Saul could see her.

"Hey Saul, got a minute?" she called out to him, and Saul, ignoring the complaints from his friends, walked off the court. When he walked up to Sandra, he wrapped his arms around her small waist and pulled her up close.

"It's good to see you again."

"It's good to see you too," giggled Sandra. She closed her eyes and puckered her lips, so Saul could kiss her.

Seeing what the naïve girl wanted, Saul smashed his large black lips against her innocent mouth. He forced his tongue down her throat, and while kissing her, kneaded her butt openly, for his friend's benefit.

"How'd you get out'ta the house?" asked Saul, once he pulled his face back to look down at Sandra.

"I ran away from home," she answered.

"So, you gonna let me tap that ass tonight?"

Sandra pulled Saul down, closer, so she could whisper in his ear and said, "Uh-huh...I want to have your babies."

"Whoa...Really...?"

Saul had not expected to hear that coming from someone so young, so he pulled back, rejecting the idea.

"What, don't you want me to have your children?"

Sandra had hoped Saul would be happy and hadn't anticipated his response. Her disappointment was evident.

"No, it ain't that. It's—"

Saul turned and looked at Annette. Deciding to change the subject, he asked, "What about your friend here?"

Sandra glanced back at Annette.

"Oh her, we're together. Ain't that right?"

Annette nodded nervously, while looking passed Sandra and Saul, to the group of young men staring at her. They were grinning like a pack of hungry hyenas.

Saul turned back and looked at his crew. He grinned.

"Ya'll keep playing. I got this..."

"Where you gonna be?" someone asked as Saul walked away with the two girls in tow.

"We'll be in the vacant house on the corner, down by Daniel's place. Ya'll come *join* us in about an hour, or so. Okay?"

#

When Daniel and the other guys arrived at the vacant house, Annette was sitting on the porch. Everyone walked passed her and on into the house, except Daniel. He sat down on the porch too.

"What'cha doing out here?"

"Nothing," answered Annette with a shrug, although she did glance back when the last person walked into the house.

"Where's your friend?"

"In there...with her boyfriend."

"Really?" asked Daniel and he immediately became concerned for Sandra's safety.

"Why don't we go inside to see what's going on?"

"I know what they're doing and don't need to see it," snapped Annette. She felt like an idiot for following Sandra.

"But you go on," she added, "If watching's your thing."

"Watching? Watching what? Are they...?"

"Yep, she—" Annette began to say, but when Sandra screamed, she and Daniel got up off the porch and rushed into the house.

"Please Saul," cried Sandra, "Don't do this!"

Saul had convinced Sandra to undress, so they could have consensual sex, but when his friends walked into the house, he said they all could have a turn with her.

When Annette rushed into the house, and saw Saul with his pants down and standing over Sandra's head, she fearlessly rushed forward and pushed him.

Saul tumbled and fell clumsily to the floor.

"Leave her alone!" cried Annette, when she saw someone had already mounted Sandra. "I said, 'Get off of her!'"

Annette rushed around the old bed and began to pound on the rapist's back, but he ignored her.

Unaware Saul had gotten to his feet and pulled up his pants, and was walking toward her; Annette continued beating on the rapist, until she was grabbed and spun around.

Saul slapped Annette, and when she fell backwards, he grabbed her blouse and ripped it open to expose her budding breast.

"Will ya' look at that, I bet she got a tight little hole?"

Sandra, still being raped, craned her head and looked in Annette's direction. When she saw Saul standing over her, she screamed, "Leave her alone you idiot, she's a virgin!"

When the others waiting for their turn heard that Annette was a virgin, they moved toward her. Annette, realizing she was next, got up and tried to run, but Saul tripped her.

"NO!" she screamed and scrambled backwards, away from Saul. When she bumped into something, Annette looked up and saw Daniel. He was standing there, petrified by what he was witnessing.

"Help me, please!" she pleaded, but when Daniel didn't respond, Annette got to her knees, and coward behind him.

Daniel lowered his head down slowly, until he saw the frightened little girl. He reached down and grabbed her arm, and he pulled her up.

"Hey, this ain't right," he said, looking directly at Saul.

"What's not right about it?" replied Saul, and to prove his point, he gestured toward Sandra. Her eyes were closed, and her legs were up in a buck. She had stopped struggling, and was moaning, which gave everyone the impression she was enjoying herself.

"She likes it."

"Yeah, well…she's a budding whore, but this child ain't. Hell, she can't be any more'n twelve."

"Come'on, you know our motto; Eight to eighty, blind, cripple or crazy!"

Saul took a step forward, so Daniel, bracing himself, prepared to defend Annette's virtue.

"Saul, I ain't standing by and letting this happen!"

"Stop it!" cried Sandra, when she opened her eyes to find Saul and Daniel squaring off. "Saul, just leave them alone!"

Saul took his eyes off Daniel, and Annette, and looked back at Sandra. She forced herself to smile and pretended she was enjoying herself.

"I won't fight no more, I promise! Y'all can do whatever you want to me. Just leave them alone!"

"No, Sandra, no—" whimpered Annette, but Daniel cut her off.

"Shish! It's either that, or they'll rape you too!"

Annette cringed, in response to Daniel's warning, and shut her mouth. When she looked across the room, she and Sandra's eyes met.

"It's okay," cried Sandra, and to prove it was, Sandra wrapped her legs around the rapist's waist and bucked wildly.

Daniel stared at Saul, and couldn't believe his friend was capable of such evil. Still, after seeing it with his own eyes, he knew they wouldn't be friends any longer; not after today.

"So," he said, and Saul turned to face him again. "What's it gonna be?"

"Fuck you and that little bitch too!" growled Saul and he walked away.

Saul walked over to the head of the *rape* line, and pushed aside the rapist that was still on top of Sandra.

"Hey!" the guy protested, but because Saul is so much larger than he, the rapist goes to the back of the line and waits for another turn.

Daniel places his arm around Annette, and turns her away from the rape scene. They walk toward the door, unmolested by the others in the room, and exit the building.

"Thank you," cried Annette, once they are outside. "I don't know what I would've done, if you hadn't of been here. I just don't know—"

"It's okay," replies Daniel. He knelt in front of the frightened little girl.

"But—" Annette, concerned for her friend, glanced back. "What about Sandra? What about her?"

"Sandra knew what she was getting into when she started going after Saul. Hell, everyone 'round here knows he's a '*bad boy,*' and so did she. But you—"

Daniel shook his head, not understanding why Annette would choose to follow Sandra.

"What could she have told you that convinced you to run away?"

"I don't know," answered Annette. She looked down at her torn blouse. "Look at me. What am I gonna do about this?"

"Don't worry; I'll take you to my house, so you can put on one of my sister's blouses before going home. After that, I don't want to see you in these streets again, hear me?"

"Uh-huh," answered Annette, and she hugged Daniel, thankfully.

#

13

Daniel waited for Vannie to open the second drawer, and not knowing which of his past friends he'd see next, he closed his eyes and steeled himself. When he re-opened them, and looked down, he saw Lisa Adkins.

Lisa was a college freshman who enjoyed hanging out with her black schoolmates, which is why she was the only white person at the neighborhood house party where she met Daniel.

Daniel thought he was a '*Mac-daddy*' back then, because he had scored with every woman he had set his eyes on. However, when he saw Lisa it occurred to him he had not bedded a white girl yet. Therefore, he felt his list of conquests was incomplete.

"Who is that?" he asked a guy leaning against the wall just inside the entrance of the house.

The guy was puffing on a joint. His eyes were closed, while he enjoyed himself, but when Daniel touched his shoulder, the pot smoker opened his eyes and quickly scanned the room. When it occurred to him, that he didn't know Daniel or the girl he was asking about, the dope head waved his hand flippantly and returned to his joint.

Determined, Daniel tapped the pot smoker's shoulder again, but this time, when he opened his eyes, Daniel pointed toward Lisa.

"Over there, who's that? Is she with anyone?"

The pot smoker turned and faced Daniel. He exhaled and blew smoke into his face.

"Man, I don't know that white gurl. Hell man," he said, obviously annoyed, "I don't even know you, so how am I s'posed to know who that silly ass white gurl's with?"

"All right brother, all right. It's cool. It's cool."

Daniel walked away, and began meandering through the crowd. Eventually, he maneuvered himself to the spot next to Lisa.

"H-e-y!" he said loudly, and tried to sound cool.

"Hey back at you!" replied Lisa. She had seen Daniel walk into the house, and was instantly smitten by his good looks, but she didn't want to appear *easy*.

"So...what's your name?"

"Huh?" Lisa touched her ear, signaling she couldn't hear, because of the loud music.

"I SAID..." answered Daniel, with an elevated voice. "WHAT'S YOUR NAME?"

Lisa turned fully around and faced Daniel. *Wow! You're a tall drink of water*, she thinks and then said, "Lisa...My name is Lisa...What's yours?"

"Daniel, but most folk 'round here call me *meat*."

Daniel had stolen the pick up line from someone else. He knew it was lame, but he hoped it would be good enough to spark a conversation, and it was.

"Meat, huh?" responded Lisa, with a smile.

Daniel looked away intentionally, so Lisa could steal a quick glanced at his crotch.

"Yeah," he replied confidently, "*Big meat!*"

Once Daniel turned to face Lisa again, he caught her averting her eyes, so he smiled. *She was checking out my package.*

He holds out his hand.

"Wanna dance?" he asked and Lisa takes it.

"Sure, why not?"

Daniel and Lisa dance wildly, until the DJ slows the music and plays a romantic ballad. Without asking, Daniel grabbed Lisa by the waist and pulls her close, and they keep dancing.

"So…Where you from?" he asked.

"Phoenix."

"Phenix City…Alabama?"

"No, silly…Arizona," giggled Lisa. "Phoenix, Arizona."

"Oh, sorry, this is the south…naturally I assumed you meant Phenix City, Alabama."

"Do I look like I come from Alabama?"

Daniel backed away from Lisa, so he could get a better look at her. When she struck a *'Model's'* pose, and Daniel saw just how *thick* she really was, he wondered if Lisa was half black, because she was *fine* and built like a *sister*.

"Naw," he answered, while pulling Lisa close again. "You don't look like one of them no teeth, country bitches."

While dancing, Daniel ground his crotch suggestively against Lisa's leg, hoping she could feel his manhood.

Oh my! Wondered Lisa, *Is that all him?*

Because of the expression on Lisa's face, Daniel knows she can feel his *meat*, and imagines she's now asking herself; *can I handle it?*

"You know," he said, "You look like one of them runway models; straight out'ta the big apple."

Lisa's face turns red. She's flattered by the comment, and continues to allow herself to be reeled in by Daniel's charm.

"Really, I was thinking of going there one day?"

"Maybe you should let me take you there."

Daniel lowered one hand and palmed Lisa's gyrating hips as if they were old lovers. Initially, his touch was light, and Lisa, had she given it much thought, probably thought it was accidental. And because of that, Daniel became emboldened. He grabbed her with both hands and began to squeeze and knead Lisa's hips.

"Are you offering to take me to New York?"

"Someday, but not tonight…baby. Tonight I want to take you to heaven."

"And what makes you think I'd let *you* take me there?"

"Because…It's my job to escort lost angels back to heaven."

"I didn't know they allowed devils in heaven."

Daniel spun Lisa around. When they stopped, he dipped her back, and while staring down into her blue eyes said, "I'm one of the good guys." He tried to kiss Lisa, but she places her finger against his mouth.

"No," she said, but then, feeling the heat of staring eyes, Lisa looked from one side of the room to the other and saw all of the other couples had stopped dancing. The other girls were staring at her, disapprovingly.

"Why'd you choose me over all of the beautiful black sisters in here? Do I look that easy?"

"No, baby..." answered Daniel, while ignoring every one else in the room. "I was drawn to you by fate."

"You're full of shit, you know that?" chuckled Lisa. She then pulled him closer and whispered into his ear.

"Got a car?" she asked.

"Yeah," answered Daniel, nodding.

"A place of your own?" asked Lisa, and she licked her tongue over Daniel's earlobe.

"Uh huh..."

A mischievous smile slowly forms on Daniel's face, because he thinks his charm has won the day. However, when Lisa pushed him back and stormed off the dance floor, he thought he had said something wrong. Confused, Daniel turned and walked over to the makeshift bar. He orders a drink. He raised it to his mouth, but before drinking it, he glanced toward the exit and spots Lisa. She's standing next to the door, waiting. When their eyes connect, she smiles, and gesturing with her finger, calls for Daniel to come outside.

Chugging the drink, Daniel pays the bartender and rushes across the dance floor to the door. Outside, Lisa's standing on the porch looking at the line of cars parked along side the street.

"Which car is yours?" she asked, and Daniel points to a sixty-five *Chevy* low-rider with suicide doors and chrome three-way knock off Craigers.

"That one," he answered, and Lisa steps off the porch and walks toward it.

"Figures," she says.

When Lisa got to his car, Daniel rushed ahead of her and opened the door.

"So you are a gentleman," she said, but Daniel didn't reply. Instead, he slammed the door, and then runs around to the other side of the car.

After Daniel got in the car, Lisa slid across the seat and snuggled up against him. Aggressively, she leaned in closer and gave him a long, wet kiss. She rested one hand on Daniel's leg and began to rub up and down on it, until she touched his crotch.

"Oh my, is that *all* you!?"

"Uh-huh."

"Really, can I see it?"

"What?" blurted Daniel, "Now?"

Daniel swiveled his head around, to see if anyone was watching, while at the same time, tried to prevent Lisa from opening his pants.

"Com'on, I can't wait!" she squealed, excited.

"Okay, but—"

Before Daniel could finish, Lisa unbuckled his belt and stuck her hand down into his pants.

"Oh gawd, that's the biggest cock I've ever seen!" she exclaimed, when she looked down.

Daniel started his car and hurrying, sped away from the curb. He drove madly, until he reached the industrial park along Camp Creek Parkway. Daniel drove around to the back of the first warehouse he came to and parked between two trailers.

#

Daniel's relationship with Lisa lasted several passionate months, but it ended painfully, because Daniel showed up at *another* house party with *another* girl. This one was Japanese. He was still trying to expand his roster.

Lisa came to the same party, and when she saw Daniel with the other girl she started a fight that Daniel had to break up.

"Lisa, go home!" barked Daniel, after pulling Lisa off of his new girlfriend. "I'll be home in a little while, so we can discuss this."

"But why can't you come with me?"

"Because…I'm gonna take him home and fuck his brains out first, that's why!" boasted the Japanese girl.

"Shut up!" barked Daniel, and the Japanese girl recoiled as if she was afraid of him. She pouted her lips.

"You're not leaving me, are you?" she asked, so Daniel placed his arm, reassuringly, around the Japanese girl's neck and pulls her close. He gave her a peck on her cheek too.

"Naw, baby…I ain't tapped that ass yet?" whispered Daniel, but then he looked over at Lisa and said, "Baby, I'll be home before you know it, promise."

"Really…?" Lisa was in love, so she ignored everything she had just seen and heard. "Then you still love me?"

"Yeah baby…really, I do."

Daniel turned, and was just about to re-enter the party, when one of Lisa's friends stepped up to him.

"You know she's pregnant, don't you?"

Daniel nodded and looked back. When he saw Lisa, she was getting into a car, and she was crying. If she was pregnant, Daniel knew it was his.

#

14

Daniel wondered about the child Lisa had bore, and he decided, then and there, to find it after he had solved this case.

"You know her?" asked Vannie, when Daniel averted his eyes and turned away from the body.

"Yeah," he answered in a weak voice.

"Pretty girl," replied Vannie, as she stared down at Lisa's body for a moment longer. When it became apparent, that Daniel was truly upset by the sight of it, she closed the drawer.

"You okay?"

"Yeah, I'm okay."

Daniel wiped his eyes with the back of his hand, and then resumed writing in his notebook.

Vannie walked back to her desk, and picked up five files. She handed them to Daniel.

"I believe these murders are all related, and committed by the same person."

"That official?" asked Daniel. "Are you going to issue these findings to the D.A.?"

"It is and yes, I am."

"When…?"

"Well, given my back log…" Vannie turned and looked at the bodies being autopsied. "It'll probably take me a couple of weeks to get it written up all '*official*' like. Is that enough time for you to do your thing?"

"My thing?" asked Daniel, and the corners of his mouth curl up slightly.

"Detective, you and I have been working together for some time now; long enough for each of us to know how the other operates."

Vannie walked over to a counter and pulled a set of rubber gloves out of the dispenser. While putting them on, she stared at Daniel and waited for his response.

"So... *is* that enough time, or not?" she asked, and Daniel extended his hand.

"Yeah," he answered, when Vannie shook it. "It is. Thanks doc."

Vannie donned her surgical mask once more and walked over to the autopsy she had been supervising, when Daniel originally came in. She walked up the step ladder, and after watching her assistant for a moment, begins to critique his technique.

# # #

15

A car sits on cinder blocks at the end of a dead end street, and serves as a testament to the decaying inner-city. With faded paint and windows covered from the inside with newspapers, it also serves as someone's home.

The inside of the car reeks with the scent of an unwashed body. There are no seats in the car and the barrier normally separating the back seat and the trunk is gone. It has been removed to allow a full sized mattress inside. Lying on that mattress, snoring like a hibernating bear, is Jeremy. He's tossing and turning, fighting off the demons pursuing him in his nightmares.

#

A hand touches Jeremy's shoulder. He screams, and flailing his arms, Jeremy runs through the dream house. He trips over something in the dark and falls. Jeremy looks around the room. He sees the older boy coming toward him in the dark.

Jeremy tries to stand. When he bangs his head on the roof of the car's interior trunk, he believes the older hit him over the head, so he curls up into fetal position and waits for the inevitable.

"Ahhhhhhh!!!!" screamed Jeremy, but when he opens his eyes, and looks up, he sees the roof of his car, instead of the stucco ceiling of the room in his dream. He signs, and falling back into his bed, thinks, *It was just a dream... just a dream.*

Sitting up, Jeremy rubbed the new knot on his head. When he looked forward, toward the front of the car, he saw sunlight coming in through his newspaper blinds. He smiled, because seeing the sun meant he survived another night.

"Good morning mister sun! Survived another one, huh Roscoe?"

However, after getting out of his car, Jeremy discovered he had not gotten through the night unscathed. Someone had paid him a visit after all, and they left him their calling card. They had tagged the outside of his car with spray paint again.

Jeremy's car was located at the dead end of an isolated road, and no one ever came there, except for the loose knit gang of teenagers that called themselves the *Hit Squad*. They got their jollies out of harassing Jeremy, but for the most part, they left him along, because he posed no threat to them or their criminal activities. And because the old car sat on the edge of their territory, they made it a point to occasionally tag it as a reminder, to him or any other gang thinking of invading their hood, of their presence.

"Damned kids, gonna make 'em pay one day, ain't that right Roscoe?"

Jeremy walked over to the steel barrel that was in the middle of his camp, and held his shivering hands over it. When he didn't feel any heat, he looked down into it and saw the wood, from the last fire, had burned completely up. So he turned and looked around the campsite for something else to burn.

There was a rotting wooden pallet lying in the brush behind Jeremy's car. He walked over to it and picked it up. When he got back to the barrel, Jeremy dropped the pallet on the ground and began to jump up and down on it. Had someone happened by, they would have thought Jeremy had lost his mind—what little there was left of it.

The smaller pieces of wood were picked and dropped into the barrel. After that, Jeremy rounded up some of the paper trash littering his campsite. He dropped all of that in the barrel too. He lit a match and tossed it in the barrel. When the fire caught on, and blazed up, Jeremy backed away and was about to sit on the old love seat next to the barrel, when he thought he heard someone, or something, yawning. He turned and saw Roscoe lying lazily on the love seat.

"Hey boy…!"

The dog wagged its tail, which brightened Jeremy's face. He picked up a small stick and shook it playfully in front of the dog.

"Wanna to play fetch?"

Jeremy tossed the stick, but the dog didn't move. Instead, it just stared curiously in the direction the stick was tossed.

"You're a dumb ass dog, you know that?" said Jeremy as he walked out, to retrieve the stick. When he returned, Jeremy dropped the stick into the barrel too.

Back at the car, Jeremy rambled around in his meager belongings, until he emerged with a worn down toothbrush and a brown bag. It contained a half empty bottle of whiskey.

Jeremy stuck the dirty toothbrush into his foul mouth and brush vigorously, until his gums began to bleed. He spit, and then opened the bottle of whisky and took a swig.

"Ahhhh shit!" he cried, and because the stinging was so painful, he blacked out.

#

16

Jeremy opened his eyes and looked around. It was dark.

"Don't let the street lights catch you outside" Jeremy recalled hearing his mother say. *"Your butts had better be in the house, before they come on, or else you're gonna get a whipping!"*

Concerned, about getting a whipping, Jeremy got up and took one step forward, but something tripped him and he stumbled to the floor.

"Oof!" grunted Jeremy. He looked down to discover his pants were still down around his ankles. His underwear is gone too.

Looking frantically around the room, Jeremy finally finds his underwear, but they're useless, because they've been torn to shreds.

With his pants pulled up, and fastened, Jeremy stumbled forward, feeling his way blindly through the dark. Once he finds the door, Jeremy pauses and listens before opening.

The floor creaks and moans. *Someone's coming!* Thinks Jeremy and panic stricken, he rushed out of the room, down the hallway, and out the exit.

#

The first person Jeremy saw, when he got home was Saul. He was sitting on the couch, innocently watching television.

"'S'up?" he asked Jeremy, "and where you been? We been looking—"

"Boy!" shouted Liller, and she rushed from the kitchen. "Where the hell you been, folk been looking all over the place for you? Lord have mercy; 'yo daddy's still out there looking for you!"

Jeremy didn't answer. Instead, he walked cautiously passed Saul.

Daniel was sitting on the couch, watching television too, when Jeremy walked into the house. He stood and followed him to the kitchen.

"In hide-n-seek, you're supposed to look for us kiddo…you little rascal."

Daniel put his hand on top of Jeremy's head and playfully tossed his hair. But when he touched Jeremy's shoulder, the boy pulled away from him, and that's when Daniel noticed Jeremy was shaking. Something was wrong.

"Momma…Jerry's shaking like a leaf on a tree," he said, and Jeremy averted his eyes shamefully, and looked down at the floor.

"What's happened to you?"

When Jeremy didn't answer, Daniel grabbed his chin, and forced him to look up. Liller touched Jeremy's forehead and said, "Well…you ain't got a fever, but you do fell clammy. Maybe you're coming down with something."

When Liller withdrew her hand, and was about to walk away, Jeremy grabbed her leg. He refused to let go.

"Momma, don't let him hurt me again! Please momma…please!"

"What are you talking 'bout? Who hurt you?"

Jeremy cast a quick glanced in Saul's direction, but quickly averted his eyes, when Saul looked at him. Liller raised her head and looked at Saul, but he whipped his head around and pretended he was still watching television.

"Who hurt you?" she asked Jeremy, while staring suspiciously at Saul.

"Some man," whimpered Jeremy, lying.

"What man?"

Daniel grabbed Jeremy's chin again and forced his head around, so he could look into his eyes. "What man?"

"Why didn't you come and help me?" growled Jeremy. He had seen Daniel through the cracks of the boarded up window, and had called out to him, but Daniel didn't stop. He just ran passed the house, playing hide-n-seek with the other children.

Daniel stood and stepped back. He looked up at Liller, surprised, and said, "Momma, I don't know what he's talking 'bout."

Then facing Jeremy again, Daniel asked, "What man? Who are you talking about?"

When Jeremy didn't answer, Daniel turned to Saul.

"You see any strangers hanging 'round the 'hood today?"

Saul shook his head and stood.

"Naw man, "I ain't seen anyone out of the ordinary."

When he moved toward the door, Daniel asked Saul where he was going.

"I'm gonna take a walk…Uh, to see if I could spot anyone I don't know," answered Saul, reaching for the doorknob.

"Hold on," replied Daniel, and Saul froze. He looked back over his shoulder to Daniel and said, "Why, what's up?"

"You don't know who you're looking for, so hold on a minute."

Daniel turned to Jeremy once more and asked, "What did this man look like? Was he white, black or Mexican?"

"I don't know…"

"You don't know? What's that suppose to mean?"

"I DON'T KNOW!" cried Jeremy. He let go of his mother's leg and ran down the hall, toward his bedroom. "YOU DON'T BELIEVE ME ANYWAY!!!"

#

17

Jeremy rose up off the ground and returned to the car. He opened the glove box, where he kept his stash, and found it empty. Apparently, the night marauders did more than *just* tag his car. They took his dope too, which meant Jeremy couldn't do anything to suppress the violent nightmares that plagued him.

A quick check of his pockets revealed to Jeremy that he didn't have any cash either, because they were empty too. So he backed out of the car and rushed around to the hood. He popped it open, and went directly to his '*secret*' stash. But when Jeremy pried the lid off the dried out looking old battery, all he found was muck. The dollar bills he had been stuffing in the old dead battery had been completely dissolved; eaten up by the acid. Jeremy thought, because the battery was dead, it was all dried out and safe for stashing paper money.

"*Told'ja...*"

"Shut up...god dam'mit!"

Jeremy looked angrily over at the dog, but when he saw it sitting up on the arm of the love seat, wagging its tail, he smiled.

"Well...then, I guess we're gonna have to go downtown and put on another show, huh?"

Roscoe, wagging its tail faster, tilted its head to one side. It turned and looked toward downtown Atlanta.

"You up to it; ain't you?" asked Jeremy, and the dog leapt off the love seat and ran excitedly out into the street. It picked up a dingy yellow tennis ball and returned it to Jeremy. Then the dog ran back out into the street and waited for Jeremy to toss it.

"Naw, chasing balls ain't gonna get us no real money. Now get out'ta the street 'fo you get run over again."

Jeremy clasped his hands behind his back, and began to pace back and forth, trying to think of a new scam.

"We need a new trick, something they ain't seen before."

Roscoe trotted back to where Jeremy was pacing and sat back on its haunches, thinking too. When his ears suddenly raised, Roscoe rose up on its back legs and began to whimper; begging.

"Naw...we done the begging routine before, so there's got to be something else...something we ain't thought of."

Roscoe dropped suddenly to the ground and rolled over onto its back. He stuck his legs into the air and let his tongue dangle lifelessly out of his mouth, pretending to be dead.

"Okay, maybe you're onto something."

Jeremy knelt beside Roscoe and poked him with his skinny finger, but the dog didn't move.

"You play dead, and then, when someone comes to help you, I can rush up behind them and knock 'em over the head with a rock!"

Upon hearing Jeremy's take, on the playing dead idea, Roscoe quickly got to his feet. He stared curiously at Jeremy.

"Now, that's the dumbest idea you've come up with thus far," the dog mumbled as it walked back over to the love seat. When he got there, Roscoe leaped up onto it and curled up into a ball.

"Well, I ain't heard you come up with anything that'll work!" snapped Jeremy as he walked over to the love seat too.

"Let's just go and sit in the park, and hold out a cup like all of the other crazies."

"I ain't crazy!" snapped Jeremy, and the dog, frightened by Jeremy's sudden outburst, scurried to the other end of the love seat.

"Yeah, right...everybody has a talking dog," replied Roscoe, once he felt he was well out of Jeremy's reach. But, without warning, Jeremy reached across the full length of the love seat and slapped Roscoe. He hit him so hard that his head came off and tumbled to the ground.

"No! No!" cried Jeremy, when he saw the headless dog sitting motionless on the love seat. "I didn't mean to do it! Why'd you have to bite me?"

# # #

18

Daniel had hoped getting Jeremy a dog would help with his depression, which is why he brought home the black pit bull terrier pup several weeks after the attack.

"Jeremy, I got something for you."

"What is it?"

"Close your eyes and I'll show you."

"I ain't closing my eyes. Someone might sneak up behind me."

"Ain't nobody—you think I'd let someone hurt you, again?"

Jeremy shrugged, but when he heard the pup yap, he looked up at Daniel and smiled.

"Is that a dog?"

"Well, I know how much you always wanted one."

Daniel held out the puppy, but before he could give it to Jeremy, the animal squirmed free of his grip, and dropped to the ground. It scurried over to Jeremy and began to lick his hand.

"See, he likes you already."

"What's his name?"

"He ain't got one yet, so I guess you'll have to come up with something."

Daniel knelt in front of Jeremy and the pup, and he scratched behind the dog's ears.

"Just don't name him something dumb, like Fido or Rex. Okay?"

"I got just the name for 'em."

"Yeah, and what's that? Capone? Scar Face? Maybe you can call him Little Caesar."

"No, those are stupid names."

Jeremy took hold of the pup's face and held it up, so he could look into its eyes. Then he said, "Roscoe."

Jeremy stepped back from the pup and patted his chest.

"Come here boy!" he called, and the pup leaped up and rested its front paws against Jeremy's small chest.

"Well, I'll be!" exclaimed Daniel, when he saw how his brother and the pup interacted.

"But why Roscoe?" he asked, so Jeremy looked up from the dog.

"Ain't that what gangsters call their guns, Roscoe?"

"Yeah but…what's that got to do with the dog?"

"I'm gonna train 'em to be my guard dog, so I can sic 'em on people who mess with me."

"Okay…I understand that, but why Roscoe?"

"Cause, I'm too young to buy a gun," said Jeremy, speaking way too serious for someone his age.

"Well…okay, yeah…" mumbled Daniel, not entirely understanding his brother's thinking. Deciding to change the subject, Daniel began to talk about the dog's care.

"Now, he'll need to be given fresh water every day, and you have to feed him."

Jeremy nodded and said, "Uh-huh…I know, and I'll walk him every day too. And after he gets bigger, I'm gonna start training him to bite people."

Daniel was still concerned, but he left the pup in his little brother's care anyway. He walked away, but when he glanced back, and saw his brother and the dog rolling around on the ground, he smiled.

"Don't forget," he called back, "I need to take him to the vet tomorrow! Okay?"

###

The following day Daniel rushed home from school, so he could take Roscoe to the vet as promised. But when he got there, and found Jeremy sitting on the porch alone, he asked where Roscoe was.

"I don't know," answered Jeremy. He was back to his old self; depressed and distant.

"What do you mean, 'you don't know'?"

Daniel scanned the yard for the dog, but he didn't see him, so he asked, "Jeremy, where's Roscoe?"

"I don't know..." Jeremy looked up, and Daniel saw he had been crying.

"What's wrong?"

"Ain't nothing wrong."

"Then why are you crying?"

Jeremy stood and wiped his eyes. He folded his arms across his chest, trying to act tough, and said, "I ain't crying."

"All right, so you ain't crying...but you still haven't told me where Roscoe is. I need to take him to the vet, so he can get his shots, or else he could get sick and die. You don't want that to happen, do you?"

Jeremy shrugged, but he doesn't answer.

"Boy, I asked you a question..." said Daniel, growing impatient. "Now, where is that dog?"

"I don't know where that dumb dog is, okay!"

Daniel walked away and headed for the back yard. When Jeremy saw where he was going, he stepped off the porch and asked, "Where are you going?"

"To find Roscoe, he needs his shots."

Daniel discovered the gruesome truth, when he walked behind the house and saw the blood. It was everywhere and appeared as though someone had chased the dog down, because its body was lying on the ground in front of its dog house, while the head was lying further out in the yard; covered with blow flies. A large butcher knife was lying on the ground too, along with a single red rose.

When Daniel heard snickering, he turned around to see Jeremy. His bloody hands were covering his mouth, but Daniel could tell he was smiling.

"Why—why would you do that?"
"Because…It bit me!"
"But did you have to cut its head off?"
"I said, 'It bit me!'"
"And you had to kill it?"
"Yes!" barked Jeremy, just before running back around to the front of the house, where he went inside and hide in his bedroom.

# # #

19

Jeremy made his way to the city center, with hopes of scoring some cash. Along the way he swiped a hand full of roses from a flower vendor, and then staked out the corner across the street from Centennial Park, next to the Omni Hotel. There he waited for the conventioneers and tourist to come out.

It wasn't long before a security guard spotted Jeremy. He ordered him to go somewhere else.

"Aw com'on…Roscoe and me just trying to make an honest buck."

"Roscoe…?"

The security guard looked around for another homeless person, but when he didn't see anyone else, he faced Jeremy again.

"Who the hell's Roscoe?" he asked.

Jeremy, gesturing to the spot on the ground beside him, said, "My dog."

"Look, I ain't got time for your bull shit tonight, so move on," said the guard, when he didn't see Roscoe.

Jeremy backed slowly away from the corner, and was about to walk away, when he spotted a couple exiting the hotel. He tipped an imaginary hat and walked across the street. He stood there, just out of the guard's jurisdiction, until the couple was well off the hotel's property. After that, Jeremy rushed across the street and tried to stop the tourist. Walking backwards, he danced to get their attention. At the end of his performance, Jeremy dropped to one knee with his hands out.

"Ta da!" he exclaimed, but the couple walked around him.

"Aw com'on, can't ya'll help a brother out? I's be a vet and Uncle Sam done kicked me to the curb. Dancing's all I got left, so please, help a brother out."

The woman, clutching her husband's arm, tried to ignore Jeremy at first, but when he lowered his head to make himself appear more pathetic, she caved.

"Honey, he's a vet…Give him a dollar."

"He ain't a veteran," groaned the husband, "And I'll prove it."

Jeremy snapped to attention, with his chest out, when the husband approached him. He raised his hand—the wrong hand—and saluted with three fingers, like a *boy scout*.

"What branch did you serve in?" the husband asked, and Jeremy opened his mouth to answer, but he suddenly went blank. He had not anticipated answering *real* questions about his military service, which was none and void.

"Honey…that's rude," said the wife, genuinely embarrassed by her husband's question, but he didn't care.

"Uh…that's okay ma'am." Jeremy sounded sad and down trodden. "I get questions like that all the time."

Looking pathetic, Jeremy lowered his head and stared down toward the ground while trying to think of an answer. When he couldn't think of one, he raised his head and shrugged.

The husband smirked, and said, "I didn't think so." He was convinced Jeremy was hustling them. But then Jeremy said, "I's be in the special services."

"Really…?"

"Uh-huh and my job was to uh…I mean, I was the one who had to check all the unexploded bombs along side the roads. You know, 'dem IUD's."

"IUD's…? What's that mean?"

"You know, that's 'dem bombs that blow up in your face. Uh…that's why I'm like this."

Jeremy tossed back his long, dirty dreads, so the couple could get a better look at his face. He contorted it and made it appear as though he was disfigured.

"One of 'dem blew up in my face," he said, and then leaning closer to the women added, "I used to be a handsome fella', but now I look like a homeless bum."

The husband snorted and chuckled, and then outright laughing, dug his hand into his pocket and pulled out a handful of loose coin. He dropped them all into Jeremy's outstretched hand.

"Here, now go and buy yourself another act. That one's stale."

Jeremy stared down at the money for a moment and then, all of a sudden, he let out a big *whoop tee doo* and started dancing.

"See Roscoe!" he said, and walked away from the coupled. "I knew it would work! Everybody wants to help a soldier!"

"Yeah...well, it almost didn't work and don't forget, that ain't folding money either, which is what we need to buy your medicine."

"I know...and my head hurts!" whined Jeremy. "We need to find a quiet place to rest; somewhere where no one will bother us."

"I know just the place!"

Roscoe trotted ahead of Jeremy.

"Follow me!"

The ghost dog led Jeremy behind the Congress Center, where it disappeared beneath a docked trailer.

"You can sleep here, while waiting for your head to stop hurting."

"What about the security guards?"

Jeremy was standing next to the trailer, looking nervously up and down the access road.

"Won't they come run us off?"

"Naw, not if you're quiet as a field mouse."

Roscoe's head rolled out from beneath the trailer and looked up at Jeremy.

"They won't suspect a thing," it added.

"Well, okay...if you say so."

Jeremy dropped to his knees, and scurrying quickly, crawled beneath the trailer. He curled up between the rear wheel axles and fell asleep.

#

20

Saul stowed his meager belongings in the overhead bin, and then sat in the empty seat beneath it. After settling back in his seat, he opened the envelope containing his release papers and read them again. A warning, in red ink, had been stamped across the top of the first page, so anyone reading the release papers would know exactly how dangerous he really was.

Banned!!! Parolee cannot travel pass Texas, or travel freely into any other portion of the western United States!

Further down the release papers were the instructions ordering Saul to report immediately to his parole officer, upon his arrival in Atlanta. And scribbled along the borders was a personal warning from the prison psychologist highlighting Saul's predilection for violence, when trying to resolve his problems. Saul had served his time, and had been given a fresh start, but his history of violence was determined to follow him back to Atlanta.

Ain't it enough I got this to remind me? Saul wondered, while rubbing his prosthetic leg. *Why they'd have to go and write this shit in my file too?*

# # #

After arriving on the west coast, Saul had hooked up with a local low life name Lee Vern. Together, they became a two man crime wave;

burglarizing homes, boosting cars, pushing drugs, and gang raping young girls. The beginning of the end for them started the night they decided to pick up a young white girl who was standing in a parking lot, waiting for a ride.

"I see one…pull over here!" exclaimed Saul, when he saw the girl.

"That white girl ain't gonna be interested in no black muthafucker like you," joked Lee Vern, but he made a U-turn and drove up to the girl anyway. While Saul rolled down his window and leaned out.

"Hey-y-y-y!" he shouted, grinning cheerfully, but the girl ignored him. When she turned and walked away he said, "Aw-w-w, com'on! I just wanna talk!"

Lee Vern stopped the car, a few feet pass the girl, and Saul got out and walked up to the girl.

"You need a ride?"

"No thank you," answered the girl, while casually sticking her hand down into her bag. "I'm waiting on a cab."

When the girl pulled her hand out of the bag, she was holding a small bottle of mace. She held it up, and with her finger on the trigger said, "I know how to use this!"

Saul held up his hands and covered his face. He quickly backed up, but in his haste, slipped on the loose gravel that covered the edge of the parking lot, and he tumbled over backwards. His feet flew up, into the air, and his back hit the ground soundly.

"Ooof!"

Still concerned he was about to get hit with the mace, Saul held up one hand and covered his eyes.

"Look lady, I was just offering you a ride. It's late and ain't no telling how long it's gonna take for a cab to show up, that's all. Shesh…"

The girl stared, suspicious, down at Saul, and even though she thought he was handsome, she said, "Thanks, but I don't ride with strangers."

Saul peeked out, from behind his raised arm, and saw the girl had lowered her mace. He smiled and then got to his feet, where he dusted off his pants.

"Okay..." he said, "my name is Saul. So there, we ain't strangers no more."

"Just like that, huh?"

"Uh-huh..."

The girl snickered and returned the mace to her purse.

"What's your last name?"

"Thompson...Solomon Thompson."

Saul held out his hand, offering it up for the girl to shake, but when she reaches for it, she saw blood. Apparently, when he fell, Saul tried to brake his fall with his hand and the gravel ripped his skin.

"You're bleeding. Are you all right?"

The girl threw caution aside and stepped closer to Saul, so she could examine his hand. She took it into her own and gently picked out the small stones that were still in the wound. Then she reached into her handbag again and pulled out another small spray bottle. It was disinfection.

"Ouch! That shit stings!" cried Saul, after the girl squirted the medicine on the wound.

"Don't wimp out on me now," she said, smiling warmly up at Saul.

"Thanks," Saul replied, and when the girl released his hand, he clinched it several times to make sure it was alright.

"You're welcome."

"You have a good bedside manner," said Saul, while looking down into the girl's smiling face. "Beautiful eyes too. What's your name?"

"Darlene."

"Just...Darlene?"

"HEY!" a voice shouted from the car, prompting Saul to look back.

Lee Vern had slid over to the passenger side, and was leaning out of the window.

"Is she coming...or what?" he shouted, "I Ain't got all day!"

"Who's that?" asked Darlene, when she saw Lee Vern leaning out of the window.

"Oh, him...? That's Lee Vern, it's his car."

"So you're offering me a ride in someone else's car? What? Did you tell him you knew me, so he would stop?"

"Something like that," admitted Saul. "Because when I saw you, standing there, looking like an angel, I had to meet you."

Darlene's face turned red, and her sense of danger passed. She leaned to one side and looked passed Saul to Lee Vern.

"Is he cool? I mean...It's safe to ride with him, ain't it?"

"You're safe with me, don't worry 'bout him."

Saul turned and began walking toward the car, but he stopped, and turned around, when he realized Darlene hadn't moved.

"You *do* want that ride, don't you?"

"You don't bite, do you?" asked Darlene, still unsure. She looked down the dark street and wondered, *where is that cab?*

"No, not really...Uh...well, maybe a little."

Saul appeared serious for a moment, but his façade quickly melts away as he chuckles.

"Hey, I'm just fucking with you!" He holds out his hand. "Com'on, it'll be fun."

Darlene accepts Saul's offer and walks over to the car. But before getting in, she bends to looks inside, and sees Lee Vern rolling a joint.

"You get high, don't 'cha?" he asked and Darlene nodded enthusiastically. "Yeah, cool! Then com'on let's go and get fucked up!"

Lee Vern held the joint out for Darlene to take. After she did, and got into the car, Lee Vern shouted, "Yahoo!"

"So, just where's the party?" asked Darlene, after she lit the joint, but Lee Vern didn't answer. Instead, he drove on without uttering another word.

While Lee Vern meandered through the city, Saul and Darlene pass the joint back and forth. At one point, Saul turned it around and put the burning end of the joint into his own mouth, and gesturing for Darlene to come closer, he gave her a *shotgun.*

"Ack...ack!" coughed Darlene and she backed away from the joint. But at that very instant, Saul grabbed her by the head and tried to kiss her.

"No, stop!"

"What's wrong, I thought you wanted to party?"

"Just stop the car and let me out."

When Lee Vern ignored Darlene's request she screamed, "LET ME OUT, NOW!"

Lee Vern slammed his foot down, and the car came to a screeching halt. The inertia tossed Darlene forward and she hit her head on the dashboard. But she fought through the pain and reached passed Saul for the door handle. When it opened, Darlene scrambled over him and fell out of the car and onto the pavement. When she stood, and looked around, Darlene couldn't tell where she was. Lee Vern had driven out of town and they were now parked along side a dark rural road. All Darlene could see was the dark asphalt, which seemed to lead into oblivion.

"Ass, gas, or grass baby…nobody rides for free."

Lee Vern was standing beside his car, with the door open. He eyes were narrow, and he appeared to have been getting high on something much stronger than weed.

"Where are we?" asked Darlene. Trembling and frightened, she looked at Saul and said, "You said I could trust you."

"Yeah, I know…"

Saul walked over to where Darlene was standing. He gently placed one hand on her shoulder.

"Look, no one wants to hurt you, but we do want to run some dick up into that fine white ass of yours."

When Darlene looked into Saul's face it changed from warm and trusting to hard and angry.

"I don't understand," she cried, "we could have gone back to my place and made love all night long…not, not this."

Saul and Lee Vern looked at each other, and then broke out into laughter, because this is what they had intended on doing all along.

Saul faced Darlene and snarling, pressed down on her shoulder and forced her to kneel.

"I don't want to make love bitch! I just want to fuck!"

"B-but…I thought you liked me."

Saul unzips his pants, and he grabbed Darlene by her hair. With brute force, he jerked her head forward, close to his open crotch.

"Open your mouth bitch, and you'd better not bite me!"

"Please...don't," cried Darlene, but her pleas only angered Saul, and becoming more physical, he slapped her.

#

After Saul finished violating Darlene, Lee Vern took his turn. Once he finished, Lee Vern pulled Darlene off the road and dumped her into the alfalfa field bordering the road.

"If you tell anyone, we're gonna find you and cut your fucking head off...you hear me?"

Darlene nodded and didn't say anything, so Lee Vern barked, "Answer me bitch!"

"Uh-huh, I hear you. I ain't gonna tell the police...I promise."

"Better not...because we got your driver's license and work ID out of your purse, so we know where you live, and where you work."

Once Lee Vern released Darlene, she curled up in a fetal position and whimpered like a wounded animal.

Lee Vern pulled out his pecker and urinated on Darlene, and then he walked back to his car and got in. After starting his engine, but before driving away, he looked over at Saul. He was reclined back in the passenger seat, smoking a joint.

"Which way you heading?" he asked, but when Saul didn't respond, he spoke louder.

"Hey, where are you heading?"

#

21

"Where are you heading?"

Saul had been sleeping, with his head leaned against the window, and did not know who it was questioning him. Once the fog cleared from his head, he looked up and saw a cute teenage girl who looked sixteen or seventeen. Her hair was red and pulled back into a ponytail. The clothes she wore openly advertised the only marketable asset she had; sex.

Still not accustomed to seeing *real* girls, Saul didn't reply initially. Instead, he just stared at the girl's boobs. But once he realized what he was doing, he quickly scanned the bus to see if anyone was watching him.

"Huh?" he moaned, when he looked back at the girl, and smiled.

"Where are you heading?" the girl repeated.

"Uh…I…Atlanta…I'm, going to Atlanta. What about you?"

The girl, having been on the lam for some time, sensed bad vibes from Saul, so she turned and looked for another empty seat, but there were none. The bus was filled to capacity.

"Louisiana," she mumbled, and reluctantly, took the seat next to Saul.

"Yeah…Where…?"

"Bat'on Rouge."

The girl pulled out her I-pod and slipped the earwig speakers into her ears. She reclined her seat, and cranked up the volume; hoping Saul took the hint, but he didn't and kept talking.

"So what's your name?" he asked, and when the girl didn't immediately reply, Saul touched her forearm.

The girl glanced down at her forearm, and saw Saul's hand hovering over it. She pulled out one of the earwigs and annoyed, said, "What?"

"I asked your name?"

Saul smiled and tried to make the girl feel at ease, but he hated being ignored.

"Mine's…Uh, Quincy…" he said, lying.

"Quincy…huh, that's funny, because you don't look like a Quincy."

Sensing Saul's deception, the girl thought it best not to tell him her real name, so she replied with "My name's Cinnamon."

Then as quickly as she could, the girl stuffed the earwig back into her ear and closed her eyes.

"So…what's in Baton Rouge, huh? Family?" asked Saul, he had turned his head and was staring out the window. When he looked back at the girl, and saw she had put the earwigs back into her ears, he reached over and yanked them out.

"I'm talking to you," he said, and Cinnamon snapped, "Hey, what's your problem, man?"

Saul, not used to being ignored, took the girl's behavior as a sign of disrespect. When she stood, and grabbed her things from the over head storage bin, Saul felt the urge to put her in her place.

"Man…you need to get a life!"

The girl stormed down the aisle and asked the first male passenger she came to, to switch seats with her.

"Please, mister…" she pleaded, "That guy's creeping me out."

The male passenger, an elderly man, nodded and without being asked twice, stood up. He stepped back, so the girl could take his seat. He blew a loving kiss to his wife and then walked down the aisle to the vacated seat next to Saul. When he got there, the old man stared at Saul.

"Look' it here, young man…" he said, "We ain't gonna have no problems, is we?"

"Naw," mumbled Saul, and disappointed, he turned his head and looked out the window. After a moment had passed, he leaned his head against it and closed his eyes.

"Good, and just so we don't get off on the wrong foot, mah' name's Joseph Musgrove; most folk call me Joe."

Joe held out his hand, but Saul ignored the friendly gesture. After Joe sat, he looked at Saul and saw the prison tattoo on the back of his neck.

"When did they release you?"

Surprised by Joe's questions, Saul opened his eyes and turned to face Joe. When he saw the faded tattoo of a teardrop beneath Joe's left eye, Saul knew he had been incarcerated too. And based on what he knew of prison culture, and what certain tattoos represented, Saul knew Joe had killed someone behind bars.

"What did you say?"

"You did just get out of prison, didn't you?"

"Is it that obvious?"

"Well, the fact that girl didn't want to sit next to you says something, don't it? And there's that tat on your neck too. They cover your entire body?"

Saul rose up, so he could glance over the top of his seat, and spotted the girl. She was engaged in a lively conversation with the elderly lady sitting next to her.

"Naw," he answered, and sat back. "Besides, I'm gonna get that one removed, first chance I get."

"That's good, because most employers won't hire a con covered in ink; scares away the customers."

Saul tapped the spot on his face, mirroring the spot beneath Joe's eye. Joe acknowledged the gesture by touching his own face.

"I keep this as a reminder…" he said, and the pain he had endured while incarcerated reflected on his face. "So I won't make the same stupid mistake again."

When Joe heard his wife's voice, he turned and leaned over his armrest, so he could look back down the aisle. He raised his hand and waved. When he turned back around, Joe was smiling.

"That ole' girl back there is my wife, Ella." Joe gestured over his shoulder with his thumb. "She's the real reason I keep my act together, so take my advice young man…find your self a good woman and settle down."

Saul considered Joe's advice. Going back to prison was something he was determined not to do again, no matter what. And like Joe's teardrop, the prosthetic leg he hobbled around on was his constant reminder.

"I remember when I was a young man…" began Joe, but having heard a multitude of old sob stories while in prison, Saul turned away and tuned out the old man. He thought about the girl that had just abandoned him, how he would get her back and teach her a lesson in respect.

"…and that's how she and I met," said Joe, completing the story.

After the driver announced they were at then end of the line, and that everyone had to get off the bus, Saul rushed into the terminal. He stood next to a bank of phone booths and waited for the girl; watching for her like a predator stalking its prey. But when Joe and Ella walk in, he noticed Ella. She was walking fast, and her hips were swaying like a hooker trying to entice a john.

"Where are you going?" Joe called out as she rushed on ahead of him.

"To find a bathroom!" answered Ella with a backward glance. As she passed the bank of phones, she noticed Saul, but kept walking.

"But we're gonna miss our connection!" shouted Joe. He had slowed his pace and was now walking.

Joe tried to catch up with Ella, but because she was much younger, he lost her in the crowd, so he stopped to catch his breathe.

When Saul saw the old man stop, he stepped away from the phone he was pretending to be using and disappeared in the crowd. He walked to the bathroom he had seen Ella duck into and walked in uninhibited.

Seeing all of the stall doors were open, which proved the place was empty, Saul walked up to the stall Ella had gone into and kicked open the door. When he saw Ella, he grinned, because seeing her there, squatting over the commode, made him realized how long it had been since he had seen a real naked women. Sure Ella was old, but she was beautiful; more beautiful than the fags he had grown accustomed to in the joint.

"Fight me and I'll kill you!"

When Saul walked into the stall, Ella opened her mouth to scream, but Saul rushed forward and placed a hand over her mouth. He spun Ella around and whispered into her ear.

"I'm gonna take my hand off your mouth, and when I do, you're not gonna say a word, are you?"

"Uh-uh," mumbled Ella.

"Good girl."

Saul slowly removed his hand. He pushed Ella forward.

"Bend over and grab the toilet head…spread your legs!"

Ella closed her eyes, knowing what was coming next. She steeled herself and parted her legs.

Saul grabbed Ella's mid-length dress and tossed it up, over her back and then, all in one motion, ripped away her underwear.

"Please…don't," she pleaded.

"Shush…it'll be over 'fo you know it."

Ella had been the first woman Saul had touched in ten years, so he finished quickly.

"That old fart must be hung like a damn mule, 'cause you're just as wide as you are deep," commented Saul, as he walked out of the stall and the restroom.

Joe, waiting patiently, smiled when he saw Ella heading toward him. After they boarded the bus, and took their seats, she laid her head on Joe's should and wept quietly.

"Honey, what's wrong?" asked Joe, but Ella doesn't answer. She knew telling him she had just been raped served no practical purpose, and would only cause undue stress in their relationship.

###

22

A dirty politician…

That's what they called Tim, after they discovered his little secret ten years ago, but was it his fault that his wife was such a prude? When she married him, didn't she vow to honor and obey? Obey? Honor? Then what the hell was she thinking when she said he could not have her any way he wanted? And the hooker, who did she think she was talking to, when she agreed to screw him; some low life street sweeper? No! He was the Mayor, and having paid his dues, expected compliance. So what if he wanted to tie her up, and '*pretended*' to rape her. She should have let him do it anyway…without question. It *was* pretend, wasn't it? What was she thinking? Couldn't she tell Tim was a *real* man with *real* urges that needed quenching? I mean really, what the hell was *she* thinking?

When he was released from Taft prison a year ago, Tim was sent back to Atlanta. The feds had offered him a ticket to Chicago, where his wife had fled after his conviction, but having gotten used to the warm southern climate, Tim refused the offer. He had acquired a taste for *Georgia Peaches*, which he knew he couldn't find in Chicago.

Politics was out of the question too, so Tim took the first job offered; working as a freight dog for the O'Sullivan Transit Company, unloading trailers delivered to the Georgia Convention Center.

Everyone on the docks knew Tim had once been the mayor of Atlanta, and they knew what he had been convicted of, so they all kept their distance from him, especially the girls. But Tim didn't care what they knew, or thought they knew, because he felt he was still better than any of the *show* floor whores free lancing their labor; installing and dismantling exhibits.

"Kelso!" barked Derrick Baker. He was one of many supervisors on the floor. "Get your potato eating ass over to dock thirty-eight, and unload that flatbed like I done told you. It's been waiting two hours!"

The show moving into the Congress Center was massive. Most of the exhibits coming in were huge and required a three stage, heavy-duty, forklift; the type Tim operated. But Tim wasn't in a hurry to do any work. He was too busy eyeballing all the female decorators, and exhibitors.

"Them trailers ain't going nowhere anytime soon, me boy. Besides, will you look'it that nice piece of ass over there?"

Tim pointed, and when Derrick saw the petite young black girl, bent over a table, he said, "She's working, which is what you're supposed to be doing. Now get your ass in gear and go to work."

Tim unbuckled his seatbelt and hopped off the forklift. Smiling, he winked at Derrick and walked away.

"I'll be right back, boss man."

"Goddam' it Tim, just where do you think you're going?" barked Derrick, but before he knows it, Tim's gone; lost in the crowd of workers. When Derrick spots him again, Tim's standing behind the decorator, ogling her butt.

"There now lassie," he says, and the decorator, startled by Tim's presence, straightened up and turned to face him.

"What'chu want?"

"Let me help you with that, why don't 'cha?"

Without waiting for the girl to accept his offer, Tim grabbed the table she was struggling with and pulled out its stubborn legs. After doing that, he sits the table up.

"There you go!" he said, slapping the top of the table, but the girl didn't say anything. Instead, she walked away.

"Hey there lassie, aren't you going to say thank you?" asked Tim, after he ran up behind the girl and grabbed her by the arm.

"Get'cho fucking hand off me!"

The girl yanked free of Tim's grasp and walked back to the cart of tables she'd been assigned to deliver.

"Don't be so mean, lassie. Me heart can't take rejection. All I want is to know your name."

"Mah name ain't your business, Mayor Kelso."

"Oh, so you know who I am?"

Tim, embarrassed, looked around and hoped no one had heard or seen the exchange he had with the girl. He had never seen the girl on the show floor before, and had hoped she didn't know who he was.

"Everybody knows who you are," she replied. "Why, did you think I was some young ignorant '*thang,*' who was just gonna roll over and let you hit it? Is that what you thought?"

"Well…Uh…actually, I…Uh…"

"So…you think I'm ignorant?"

"No. I just thought you were pretty, that's all. Call me old fashion, but I don't think pretty girls should be doing this type of work. It's too physical and labor intensive."

"You…you think I'm pretty?" asked the girl. She looked down at the dirty trousers she was wearing, and brushed away some invisible dirt. When she looked up, she was smiling.

"Yeah…not that it matters," replied Tim as he, feeling rejected, walked away and heading back to his forklift.

When Tim arrived at his forklift Derrick was still there; sitting on his yellow cart, waiting.

"That's what you get, you dumb fuck."

Derrick had been watching Tim and the girl, and he heard her put him down too.

"Now get your ass in gear, and go unload that truck, like I said."

"Fuck you," mumbled Tim, as he got back on the forklift.

"What'd you say? What was that?"

"I said 'fuck you!'" answered Tim, fearlessly. "Why? What are you gonna do about it?"

Derrick got off his cart and walked over to where Tim was sitting. He leaned into the forklift's safety cage, and through clinched teeth, said, "I don't care who you used to be and I don't care what strings you pulled, to get this gig. If you ever speak to me in that way again, I'm gonna pull you off that lift truck, and kick your Irish ass. You hear me?"

"Yeah…You and what army…fat boy?"

Tim popped his clutch and the massive machine lurched forward. Derrick jumped back, and because of the debris on the floor, nearly fell over.

"Watch out, boss man!" shouted Tim as he drove away, "This is a heavy forklift traffic area!"

Tim sped down the main aisle, and was just about to turn a corner, when he heard someone yelling. Thinking it was Derrick, he made the turn and was about to drive on, when he looked back to see the young girl he had been flirting with. She was running toward him, holding out a piece of paper.

"Wait!"

"What do you want?" asked Tim, once the girl caught up and was standing next to the forklift. "I've got to go to work and ain't got time for any of your drama."

"They're cutting the decorating crew at six," said the girl.

"Yeah, so…?"

The girl handed the paper to Tim and walked back to her table cart, before he could say anything else.

Tim unfolded the paper, and then looked up, surprised, because the girl's phone number was scribbled on it, along with her name.

# # #

23

Becky Randall was staring down into a microscope lens; when Daniel walked into the lab and asked to speak to her.

"Give me a minute, will you?" She pointed to a chair next to the door without looking. "Take a load off."

"Hurry, I ain't got all day."

Becky glanced up, but she didn't say anything in response to Daniel's comment. Instead, she picked up a pen and scribbled something in her notebook. After that, Becky calmly removed the specimen from beneath the microscope's lens and returned it to the refrigerator at the end of the room.

"Okay, what's eating you?" she asked, but when she walked up to Daniel, he held up the newspaper he had gotten from Captain Peterson.

"Yeah, I saw it…so what?"

"So what…?"

Daniel shoved the paper into Becky's hands.

"How'd they get this picture and which of your techs told 'em about that rose?"

Becky stared down at the picture for a moment, but all she focused on was her unruly hair. In the photo it looked as though she had been sleeping on her office couch, which probably wasn't far from the truth.

"I don't know…Why?"

She looked up at Daniel and shrugged, but then a curious expression appeared on her face.

What…? You think I'm the leak?" she asked, and growing angry because of Daniel's accusations, Becky tossed the paper back to him. She walked over to her desk, and picked up her camera. When she returned, Becky handed Daniel the camera.

"I ain't even downloaded the damn pictures from the crime scene yet."

Daniel looked down at the camera, and Becky pointed toward the memory card that was still in the camera.

"See…it's still sealed, just like it is before going to a crime scene. It's not unsealed, until there are two techs present to authenticate the photos."

"But—" said Daniel, not understanding how the picture could have gotten out and into the newspaper.

"—where are they getting their information?" asked Becky, finishing Daniel's question. "Hell…I don't know, but like I said, it ain't coming from me or my team."

"Okay, I believe you…"

Daniel turned to leave, but stopped and faced Becky again. There was an apologetic expression on his face, but he didn't apologize.

"You got anything else?" he asked, maintaining his investigative mode.

"Well…either this guy is a psychopathic killer, with a genius IQ, or he's one lucky son-of-a-bitch, because he ain't leaving anything behind."

"Do think it's the same person?"

"Yeah, I do…" answered Becky, confidently, but then she hesitated.

"What? Don't keep me in suspension…Speculate…tell me why you think it's the same person."

Becky picked up a folder and read silently for a moment. When she looked up, she held out the folder, so Daniel could see the pictures it contained.

"Look at the wounds on the victim's neck," she said and began flipping through the pictures. When she came to those of Annette and Lisa, she said, "I got these pictures from the coroner's office."

Daniel raised his head and stared curiously at Becky. There was a question on his mind, but before he could ask it, Becky added, "Vannie and I have come to the same conclusion. These wounds were created by the same weapon, probably a serrated knife with a sharp cutting edge."

"Anything else…Fingerprints…DNA…A fuck'n sketch of the doer…something, anything to identify this guy?"

"Well…" Becky moved over to her computer. "I did manage to pull a partial fingerprint from the note we found in Terrie Armstead's apartment."

"Any hits?"

"No, it's not in any of our data bases. Like I said, this is a genius psychopath or he's just one lucky son-of-a-bitch, and he's never been busted. One thing's for sure though…"

"What's that?"

"He's a seasoned killer. I'd bet the farm he's been doing this for years. He likes it and won't stop, until he's forced to stop."

Having heard enough, Daniel walked toward the exit again and just as he stepped through the threshold, he said, "Let me know if you come up with anything else."

"Where you off to?" called out Becky.

"I've got a couple of leads to follow up on, but don't worry I'll keep you in the loop. I got a feeling this joker's gonna strike again."

"Hey, don't you want to know about the roses we've found at the crime scenes?"

Daniel turned around, but he kept walking backwards.

"Is there something special about them?" he asked, and Becky shook her head.

"Naw, they're just your typical, run of the mill, rose. Any number of florists would carry them."

"Can we trace their origin back to a specific florist?"

"I'm good, but not that good. I'll call around, but I don't think it'll lead to anything."

"Okay, but I wouldn't waste too much time on that. I'd much rather you focus on the fingerprint, the weapon, and what DNA you've found, so we can build a case for when we catch this fucker."

"Okay…," replied Becky, as she walked back to her microscope with another specimen.

# # #

24

Saul's parole office was located in a dying strip mall off Riverdale Road, in Clayton County. The huge anchor store had moved out of it to greener pastures in the suburbs a long time ago. When he walked into the office, Saul signed in and immediately, was told by the elderly receptionist sitting behind the metal desk to take a seat. However, when Saul glanced back over his shoulder and saw all of the seats had been taken, he faced the receptionist again.

"Where?"

"Excuse me?" she replied, and sounding annoyed, she looked up. "What did you say?"

"Where should I sit?" repeated Saul, fearlessly. He gestured back toward the seating area with his thumb.

The receptionist didn't care, that was obvious. She shrugged and gestured for Saul to get away from her desk.

"Okay then…How long is the wait?" he asked, "Because, if it's gonna be a while, I'm gonna step outside and have a smoke."

"You're not allowed to leave the building," replied the receptionist, quickly and full of authority.

"What do you mean; I'm not *allowed* to leave the building?"

Saul's expression turned hard and he scowled, because the receptionist had made him feel as though he was still a prisoner.

"Just move away from my desk," she said, feeling justified in not answering Saul's question.

When Saul didn't move, the receptionist reached beneath her desk and nervously fingered her panic button.

"Where?" asked Saul, determined. "Then if I can't go back outside for a smoke, can I smoke in here?"

"This is a non-smoking building."

"Shit!" groaned Saul. He turned to look back at the waiting area.

"Please…watch your language, young man."

"Look lady…" Saul turned and faced the receptionist. "Don't tell me what to do, okay? I've had enough of that shit already."

The receptionist, concerned for her safety, pressed the button. She stood and backed away from the desk.

"Oh, I get it…" Saul said, understanding. "You called for help, didn't 'cha? Think I'm gonna hurt 'cha?"

Saul raised his hands abruptly, and the receptionist, thinking he *was* going to hit her, recoiled backwards and almost fell over. Saul chuckled as he interlocked his fingers behind his head and spread his legs. He knew the drill.

A few moments later the windowless door, leading into the back of the facility, opened and several armed men rushed out. They swarmed up to Saul, and wrestled him to the floor. Once handcuffed, they lifted Saul to his feet and escorted him to the holding area behind the door.

#

"You Saul Thompson?" asked a voice, from somewhere within Saul's tormented dreams. He opened his eyes and looked up to see a short baldheaded man.

"Yeah, that's me. Who you…my P.O.?"

"That's right! My name's Jeff Oliver," replied the bald man. He laid the file he held on the bench next to Saul, and reached for the key ring dangling from his belt.

"Squeaky wheel gets the oil, huh?" asked Jeff, while unlocking Saul's handcuffs. After that, he picked up the file and walked away. "Follow me."

Saul rubbed his wrist as he stood and walked behind Jeff.

"Man, I didn't do nothing to deserve being locked down like that. I got rights too, you know?"

Jeff stopped abruptly, and spinning on his heels, faced Saul.

"Listen to me; because I not gonna say this twice, and to be clear, you don't have *any* rights while on parole. The only difference between being on parole and being locked up, are the bars."

"What's that s'pose to mean?"

Jeff stepped closer to Saul, so he'd know he wasn't afraid or intimidated by his size.

"It means you do what I say, when I say. Understand? Now shut up and follow me."

"Where are we going?"

"You need to take a piss test."

"What! Why? I just got off the damn bus…ain't had time to score anything."

"While on parole, you're subject to random urine test; day or night, so get use to it. You're also required to submit a blood sample once a month."

"What…don't you want a stool sample too?"

"Listen, don't be a smart ass. I hate smart asses."

"Man, this shit sucks," groaned Saul, when Jeff handed him a plastic cup.

Saul took the cup and walked into the restroom. He went to close the door, but Jeff blocked it.

"I have to watch," he said, with a shrug.

"You ain't no fag, is you?"

"I can't tell you how many times I've heard that before. Look, we all have rules to follow, and this is one of mine. Now go on and get it over with, so we can sit and talk."

After Saul finished, he handed Jeff the warm cup of urine. Jeff sealed it and then, he took a pen and wrote Saul's ID number on the label. The specimen was deposited into a box, along with several others, where it waited for a courier to pick it up.

Once they were at Jeff's desk, Jeff documented his thoughts down in Saul's personal file, regarding their initial meeting; including the fact Saul had to be subdued and secured to a bench.

"Man, why you got'ta write down that shit, huh? Can't a brother get a break? You know I wasn't no threat to that old lady."

"Yeah, I know…" replied Jeff, but he kept writing dutifully.

"Then why are you documenting it?"

"Just doing my job…just doing my job."

Jeff looked up and noticed Saul scratching his thigh; just above the prosthetic he wore.

"How much did they cut off?"

"Just below the knee," answered Saul, with a quick rap against his fake leg.

"Says here; you were shot in that leg and it had to be cut off, because gangrene set in while you were in the prison infirmary. That right?"

"Yeah…"

Jeff closed the file and sat back in his chair.

"So…who shot you?" he asked, and Saul, angered because of the question, snapped, "You know damn well who shot me, so why you questioning me about it?"

"I know what it says in here…" Jeff tapped his pencil against the file. "But it doesn't tell me everything and I like to know who I'm dealing with. I want to know everything about you, or as much as I can. In return, I'll tell you about me."

Saul eyed Jeff suspiciously, while considering him. He leaned back in his chair, and testing his boundaries, pulled out a pack of smokes.

Jeff snatched the pack from Saul's grasp. He shook out two cigarettes, but instead of giving one to Saul, he placed them both between his lips. When he pulled out the lighter, and lit the cigarettes, Saul said, "I thought this was a non-smoking office."

"It is…out there," answered Jeff, gesturing toward the front of the building. "But back here, I can do anything I want. Hell, I can even let you light up, but I wouldn't recommend doing that, because I just may give you a piss test afterwards."

A wry smile formed on Jeff's face. He winked, and then handed one of the cigarettes over to Saul.

"I guess you'll do," said Saul, taking the cigarette.

"I know that file only summarizes my criminal history, more specifically, the crime that sent me to prison..." he adds, "But that ain't the end of the story."

"Really...then tell me your story," prompted Jeff.

Saul took another drag from his cigarette. When he exhaled, he blew out several perfectly formed smoke rings.

"After arriving in Cali, I fucked around and met a girl...*thee* girl. Her name was Lupe Del Toro..."

#

Lupe was a beautiful Hispanic girl. She had long flowing black hair, and as fate would have it, got pregnant with Saul's first child soon after they began having sex. And despite the fact he was a career criminal, she agreed to marry Saul. Unfortunately, one day while they walked down the street, a car stopped in front of them, and two men jumped out brandishing guns. One, without hesitation, shot Saul in the leg.

The assassin walked up to Saul and stood over him, intending to shoot him in the head. But he hesitated, because Lupe threw her body over Saul and pleaded for his life.

"Please, don't kill him!" she cried, while blatantly displaying her large belly.

"Move out of the way, baby!" groaned Saul, showing no fear. He reached for the gun he normally kept tucked in his belt, but remembered; Lupe had begged him not to carry it in her presence.

"You know who I am?" asked the assassin, while pressing his gun against Saul's temple.

"No...I don't know you."

"Then you should' a thought about that, before raping my sister!" shouted the assassin, and he slapped Saul with the back of his hand. Then he lowered his gun and fired another round into Saul's leg.

"Arrrghhh!" cried Saul, while Lupe maneuvered her body around, so she was in front of the gun.

"Please, don't kill him...we got'ta baby coming!" she pleaded, so the other assassin grabbed his older brother's arm and pulled him back. When the older brother looked back, the younger brother pointed to the people watching.

"Cedric," he said. "Don't kill 'em! They're too many witnesses around!"

"Naw Elmo, he's got'ta pay! Else folks 'round hea' will think we're weak."

"You done dealt with it man!" shouted Elmo, tugging Cedric's arm. "Look at 'em, his leg's nearly blown off. He ain't ever gonna walk again!"

Cedric pressed the barrel of his gun against Saul's head again. This time Saul, afraid he was going to die, pulled back.

"If I ever see you again, I'm gonna kill you." Cedric rubbed his hand over Lupe's pregnant stomach. "You should thank this taco bending whore, because if she wasn't here, I would have killed you right off."

Cedric holstered his gun, and then, he fearless walked back to the car and got in, they drove away.

"...when I came too, I was in the hospital, handcuffed to the bed. Apparently, the girl I raped reported it, despite our threats, and the police collected DNA samples from her. After that, all they needed was someone to match it to."

"What about your accomplice, they ever catch him?"

"Who...The po po?"

"Who else...?"

"Oh...I thought you meant those nigga's who shot me."

"So...*somebody* did get your boy?"

"Yeah...somebody did, but I don't know who," answered Saul. "He was found in his cell; hung by a bed sheet. The coroner said it was a suicide."

"What about the ones who shot you? They ever get caught?"

Saul snickered, but he didn't answer Jeff's question. Instead, he wondered how his bitches were faring in prison, without his protection.

Cedric and Elmo, criminals in their own right, were arrested for trafficking in cocaine and sent to the Taft prison too. When Saul found out they were in the pre-detention diagnostic wing, he immediately put out the word they were his property, and arranged for them to be *turned out*.

"Well, you know what they say…what goes around, comes around."

"So…you did get them back?"

"Let's just say the scales of justice have been balanced, and leave it at that."

Jeff pursed his lips, while pondering Saul's response. He noted the cryptic comments in the file. When he looked up from it, Jeff noticed the smirk on Saul's face.

"Okay," he said, and closed the file. "The program works like this… You'll need to find a job. It doesn't have to be anything special, and with your record, I doubt you'll find anything paying much more than minimum wage. Still, you've got to demonstrate how you're supporting yourself. Okay?"

Saul blew out another smoke ring.

"Anything…just as long as it ain't illegal, right?" he asked.

"Yeah, that's right. Legal."

"Can I start my own business?"

"And how are you proposing to do that? You got some money stashed away somewhere?"

"Naw man, but I still have contacts."

"Look, it's best to stay away from old friends, especially anyone that's got a criminal record. Doing so constitutes a violation of your parole. Understand?"

"Yeah, I understand."

"What type of business were you considering, anyway?"

"I was thinking about real estate; buying and flipping houses, something like that."

Jeff eyed Saul suspiciously, and Saul, trying not to appear transparent, took another drag from his cigarette.

"Okay then..." replied Jeff. "I want to see a business proposal, including names and numbers of potential investors, when you return for your next appointment. If everything is on the up and up, I'll sign off on your venture."

Saul stood and extended his hand to Jeff.

"You know," he said, "I've never ask for anything from anyone...other than opportunity, which is what you just gave me. Thanks brother."

Jeff smiled, but he couldn't help but to wonder what it was Saul was really up to. Because in all the years he had been a parole officer, no con had ever wanted to start a business, unless it was selling drugs or hooking.

"Just get that proposal together and we'll see what happens from there; no promises, and here..." Jeff handed Saul his business card. "Call me if you have any problems, and I don't care how trivial. And don't let me get a call from the police, okay? Hear me?"

Saul took the card. He looked at it, and then holding it against his head, committed it to memory.

"Thanks...boss man," he said and stuffed it into his pocket.

"If you have any contact with the police, call me *before* they do, and I mean that."

"Okay."

"I mean it..."

"Okay," repeated Saul, with false sincerity

"Alright, now get out of here. Go back out the way you came."

Saul walked out of Jeff's cubicle, down the hall, and out the door he was escorted through. Just as he strolled passed the receptionist, Saul tapped her desk and when she looked up, he winked at her.

"See ya' around," he said, cryptically, sending chills down the old lady's back.

#

Georgia is noted for its hot, humid weather, and because of the demand, the power companies in the region are notorious for increasing their rates during the summer. Saul knew this, and hoping the receptionist slept with her windows open, he hung around the strip mall, until she got off work. And he followed her home.

When he got off the bus, Saul spotted a group of knuckleheads and thugs, hanging out on the corner, down the street from where the receptionist lived. He casually walked over to them, and although he didn't know any of them, struck up a conversation. He learned to do this while in prison.

Saul was confident none of the locals would talk to the police, or even remember him, if they were questioned, because they were all up to no good too; selling drugs, pimping, whoring, and just generally, hustling.

When the lights went out in the old lady's house, Saul glanced down at his watch. It was ten o'clock in the evening; still too early to make a move, so he waited. And while waiting, one of the local slingers approached Saul and tried to sell him some crack cocaine.

"I don't smoke that shit, but if you got some weed, I'll take some of that."

"I don't sell gateway, but Tut does."

The slinger turned and pointed to the heavy set dark figure, at the end of the street, leaning against a stop sign.

"Thanks," said Saul, and he walked away. When he arrived at the end of the street, he walked up to Tut and said, "Got that gateway?"

"I know you?" asked Tut, staring suspiciously at Saul.

"Slim, over there, said you selling…is you?" Saul gestured toward the crack dealer.

"You ain't a cop, is you?"

"Naw man…Look, you selling or ain't you?"

While Tut and Saul talked, every one of Tut's potential customers walked passed him and headed for the crack dealer. So, deciding nothing from nothing leaves nothing; Tut said, "How much'cha need?"

"Gimme a joint."

"What—a joint? Mutha' fuck 'a…I don't get out'ta my bed for a joint?"

"What…you got a minimum purchase requirement?"

"Damn Skippy!" answered Tut and he pulled a small plastic bag out of his pocket. "This is the smallest amount I sell, rolling papers are extra."

"How much…?"

"I can let you have it for twenty-five bucks."

Saul hands over two twenties as he snatches the bag, and rolling papers, from Tut. He wanted to end the transaction, because he was worried the scene Tut had created would help someone remember him.

"Hey!" called out Tut, when Saul walked away without getting his change. "You forgot your change!"

Saul waved his hand and kept walking.

# # #

It was three in the morning, and Saul stood outside the fence surrounding the old receptionist's house puffing on a joint. Once he finished it off, and began to feel the effects of the narcotic, he quietly opened the gate and walked up to the open bedroom window, where he took out his knife and slit the screen.

The old woman felt the hand on her mouth. When she opened her eyes and looked up, she saw Saul hovering above her. He was grinning.

"Yeah bitch, it's me."

The old woman tried to fend off Saul, but he was too big and determined to right the injustice and humiliation, he had experienced while shackled to the bench. Unemotional, and without empathy, Saul sliced open the old woman's throat and destroyed her ability to scream for help. After that, he removed his hand from her mouth and sat back; watching, amused, while she struggled to breathe. He reached into his pocket and pulled out a single rose. He held it up, so the old woman could see it.

#

While standing at the front door, Saul cracked it open slowly and peeped out. When he saw Tut, still standing on his corner, he shouted, "Hey! Got anymore of that weed?"

Saul walked out of the house, through the front door, and across the street toward Tut. He put his arm around Tut's shoulder and lead him away from the stop sign, around the corner to the entrance to the alley, behind the receptionist's house.

"How much of that shit you got?" he asked and Tut smiled, happy to make the sale.

"Two ounces…but I can get more," replied Tut as he dropped down to one knee and pulled up his pant leg. He kept his stash strapped to his ankle.

"What you want for it?" asked Saul, while looking around to see if anyone was watching. He pulled out his knife.

"I need five hundred yards for each—" began Tut, but before he could finish, Saul plunged his knife down, into the top of his head.

#

25

Tut's body was deposited into a recyclables bin, that several days later, was taken back to a recycling center. When one of the workers at the sorting plant detected the putrid odor of decaying flesh, he called the police. However, because Tut was a known corner dealer, his death wasn't a high priority, and was assigned to Robney.

The first thing Robney did when he arrived at the sorting plant was get a copy of the driver's route. He cross-referenced that against Tut's known hangouts, which led him to the Glen Oaks projects on Highway 92, and that's where he parked his unmarked car and waited.

# # #

Normally, Glen Oaks is alive with activity at three A.M., but today the Zombies—junkies and crack heads—suspected something and stayed away. However, Mont didn't know that, because he had been sleeping all day. So when he showed, and didn't see anyone, he immediately became concerned and was about to move on, until he saw someone shuffling down the street toward him. But as the crack head approached, Mont realized he didn't know him.

"Do I know you?" he asked, but when the man held out a wad of money, Mont ignored his tingling street senses and reached for it.

"What'cha need?" he asked, but when Mont took the money, the crack head slapped handcuffs on his wrist.

"Got'cha!" exclaimed Robney, and with minimal force, he twisted Mont's arm around his back. He grabbed Mont's other hand and cuffed it too.

After patting Mont down, Robney found a packet of crack filled vials in his pocket.

"Is this your regular spot?" asked Robney, turning Mont around, so they're facing each other.

"Man I don't know what you're talking 'bout. That shit ain't mine. You planted it in my pocket."

"Listen stupid, I ain't got time for a small time peddler like you, so if you answer my questions, I might let you go."

"Questions…what questions?"

"Is this your regular spot?" repeats Robney, but before answering, Mont looks back over his own shoulder. If he was going to talk, Mont wanted to make sure no one could finger him as a snitch.

"Yeah man, this is my spot." Mont turned to Robney. "Why? What's it to you?"

"You know a gateway peddler…goes by the handle '*Tut*'?"

"Tut? Yeah, I know 'em."

Mont bobbed his head and gestured toward the end of the street.

"That's his corner over there."

"Well, that's an open corner now, ain't it?"

"What's that 'pose to mean?"

"Ain't you heard? Tut's dead. Found his body yesterday; stuffed inside a trash bin. Know anything about that?"

"Naw man, I don't know nothing 'bout nothing."

"Is that right?"

Robney reached inside the packet and pulled out several vials of Mont's crack cocaine. He dropped one onto the sidewalk and stepped on it.

"What's it cost you to buy these?" he asked, but when Robney looked up and saw the concern on Mont's face, he knew they weren't his.

"You were *fronted* these, weren't you?"

When Mont didn't answer him, Robney dropped another vial. But this time, to emphasize his point, he stomped down hard and ground his foot into the sidewalk. When he raised his foot, all that remained of the vial, glass and all, was a small spot.

"C'mon man, that shit ain't necessary. I'm just a working stiff; trying to feed my family."

"Then tell me what I need to know!" spat Robney. He stepped closer to Mont and waited.

Mont didn't want to go to jail, but he didn't want to be labeled a snitch either, he didn't want to end up like Tut; dead. The drugs had been fronted to Mont on credit and he knew he would have to pay for them; one way or another.

"Look man, the last time I saw Tut he was standing on that corner…selling grass, as usual."

"When was that?"

"I don't know…couple nights ago, I guess."

"Did he have a beef with anyone?"

"What?"

"Did he argue over a sale with anyone?"

"Naw…not that I remember, besides, most folks in this neighborhood mind their own business. Watching what others are doing can get you killed, if you know what I mean?"

"Yeah, I know what you mean."

Robney let out a sigh of frustration. He turned and looking around, wondered why there was no one else around.

"Where's everyone?"

"I don't know, maybe that funky odor waffling through the air ran 'em off."

"Odor…What odor?"

Robney held his nose up and inhaled deeply, and for the first time, detected the odor Mont mentioned. Something was dead.

"How long that stench been in the air?"

"Man, I don't know. I don't come out 'til two in the morning. Hell, I didn't even know Tut was dead, 'til you told me. Besides, it's probably just a dog or cat."

"Yeah...maybe," laminated Robney, and because he was a dog lover, he hoped it wasn't a dog.

"Tell me," he said, returning his thoughts back to his investigation, "Have you seen anyone new hanging around lately?"

"No..." answered Mont, but when Robney moved to drop one more vial, he blurted, "WAIT! Hold on, come to think of it, there was some new dude on the block the other day. I tried to sell him something, but he wasn't interested; said he wanted weed, so I referred him to Tut."

"What else?"

"What else? Hell...ain't no *what else*!"

Mont held up his handcuffed hands.

"That's all I got, so let me go."

"Hold on a minute," replied Robney, while staring down the street, toward the corner Tut worked. He looked at the numbers on the street sign, and thinking they looked familiar, pulled out his notebook. Under the light of the street lamp, Robney read the address of the recycle bin's owner. It was the house on the corner.

"Hum?" he said, and looking at Mont again, asked, "When was the last time you remember seeing Tut?"

"I don't really recall the time, but I do know, I don't recall seeing him beyond a couple days ago."

When Robney faced Mont again, the drug dealer, still thinking he was going to be released, held up his hands.

"Can you describe that new guy?" asked Robney, but when Mont said, "Naw man, it was dark," he looked up at the street light.

Mont lowered his hands and looked up too.

"What'cha looking at?"

Robney rushed forward and grabbed Mont by his throat, and he squeezed off his air.

"Don't bullshit me," he snapped, "I know you got a good look at him, because you were standing right here, beneath this light. Now tell me... was he tall or was he a midget? What color was his hair and eyes? Was there anything distinguishing about him? A scare, a tattoo, a limp, anything?"

"Wait! That's it!" cried Mont, after Robney relaxed his grip. "He limped when he walked…as if he had a fake leg."

"Anything else…?"

"He was a big man."

"Big? Big how…tall big or fat big?"

"I don't know…average height, but he was wide across the shoulders. Looked like he'd been lifting weights for a long time, and he was black."

"African-America…? Okay, now we're getting somewhere."

"Naw, you don't understand. He was black, black as the ace of spades, but his teeth were white. Not yellow, like most of the dope heads hanging 'round hea'. They were pearly white."

Robney scribbled several of Mont's comments down, before putting his notebook back into his pocket. Then he grabbed the dealer's skinny forearm and walked him over to his car.

"Ain't you gonna let me go?"

"You're really stupid, aren't you?"

"Huh…?

"You're a drug dealer and I'm a detective, dumb ass."

"But…You said, if I helped you, you would let me go."

"My point exactly…stupid and naïve, now get in the car and shut up. I'll be back in a minute."

Robney opened the car door and shoved Mont inside.

"Where you going?" called Mont from the car, and after Robney walked away he shouted, "You can't just leave me here unprotected! This is a dangerous neighborhood!"

Robney ignored Mont's protest and walked on down the street; toward the corner. When he got there, Robney stood next to the stop sign and looked around; first in one direction and then in the other. He saw the entrance to an alley and walked over to it. When he saw the open gate, leading to the receptionist's house, he thought there was nothing unusual about the house, or the open gate. But just as he was about to close it and walk away, Robney notice there was a hole cut into the screen covering the bedroom window. He walked through the gate, and up to the back door, where he discovered it was ajar, so he pushed it open.

"Police...! Is anyone here?"

Robney walked on into the house, but hesitated, after detecting the odor of decaying flesh. He pulled out a handkerchief to cover his mouth and nose, and then he moved deeper into the house. Fighting the urge to puke, Robney walked into a bedroom where he blindly rubbed his hand against the wall, searching for the light switch. When he hit the switch, and turned on the light, he saw the old lady's decomposing body.

#

"Is that the doer?" asked Becky, when she saw a patrolman transferring Mont from Robney's car to his own.

"No, but he saw who did it."

"Really, then why's he under arrest?"

"Right now, I got him on possession with intent, but what I need is for you to put him in front of a sketch artist before he bails out. He's seen the doer, and I need to know what he knows."

"Okay, but you should know this crime scene looks familiar."

"Familiar...?"

Becky hesitates, but then realizing she's already said too much, she turned and walked away.

"Maybe I shouldn't say."

"Look, if you know something, you need to tell me."

"Well...that rose you found, it's similar to those found at the *Rose Murder* crime scenes."

"The Rose Murders...?"

"Yeah..."

"Who's the primary?"

"Detective Rose."

"Daniel?"

"Yeah...You two should talk, compare notes."

"Just get me that sketch, will you?"

"Okay, but do you want me to share my findings with Detective Rose?"

"No!" Robney blurted and cast a backward glance at Becky. "I'll share it with him, if it pans out."

"Okay, okay," replied Becky. "I should have something in a couple of days."

# # #

26

Driving down Florence Boulevard, toward his old neighborhood, was like being in a time machine for Daniel. He had not visited it in some time, and didn't recognize it anymore. Some of the old landmark stores had been torn down, while others had been boarded up. The working class neighborhood, once beautiful and clean, had been a victim of *white flight*. The properties had been neglected, while winos and homeless bums populated vacant buildings. Hookers and deviants wandered the streets at night; looking for action. Garbage overflowed into the gutters too, because the city had long ago turned the neighborhood's municipal service over to a privately own company, and their fees were expensive. Mosley Park was the place where Daniel, Saul, and every other young person, hung out back in the day. So when he turned down Pueblo Drive, and drove toward it, Daniel hoped Saul would be there. But none of the old heads were around, and all Daniel saw were just a few teenage boys, playing basketball against a one armed man.

    The sight of the old asphalt court reminded Daniel of days gone by, causing him to smile. The place hadn't changed. The basket's rims were still net-less, and the court still looked as though someone had dumped off the asphalt as an afterthought. And even after all of the years had passed, no one thought to paint boundary lines around the perimeter, or a free throw line. The girls that stood along the edge of the court, watching the boys, looked just like they did back in the day. There were several young children playing at the other end of the court, and the sight of them reminded Daniel of the day he and Saul bumped heads.

#

They were playing *three-on-three* at one end of the court, while the children were all playing '*horse*', at the other end. When some boys from a neighboring subdivision showed up, and challenged Saul, Daniel, and the others, to a game, Saul accepted it without consideration of anyone else. When he was reminded of the children using the other end of the court, he told them to go and play somewhere else.

"But we were here first!" cried one little boy, and thinking that was enough, the boy kept on dribbling the ball he played with.

"God dammit!" barked Saul. He snatched the ball from the boy, and drop kicking it, catapulted it to the other side of the park. "Now get the hell out'ta here!!"

"That ain't fair! We were here first!"

Saul raised his hand, and was about to slap the boy, until Daniel yelled for him to stop

"You say something to me?" asked Saul, when Daniel approached him.

"Yeah, I said leave 'em alone. We can play half court."

Saul shoved the boy, and then turned to face Daniel. His large black lips parted slowly to reveal his yellow teeth.

"What, you standing up for these rug-rats?"

"This is the only court in this neighborhood," replied Daniel, and thinking Saul could be reasoned with, said, "So let's be fair about it, okay? Besides, the kid's right, they were here first."

"This is my neighborhood!" barked Saul, thumping his chest with his fist. He stepped closer to Daniel and said, "Unless you're challenging me for the crown?"

Daniel didn't reply, but he didn't back down either.

"Well, are you challenging me?" asked Saul, speaking loud, so everyone could hear him.

"Saul—" Daniel was upset with himself, for opening his mouth. "—Look…Just let the kids play on that side of the court, that's all I'm saying."

"HELL TO THE NAW!" barked Saul, and Daniel, reacting impulsively, punched Saul in the jaw. He stepped back and waited for Saul to rush him, but Saul didn't move.

Saul was shocked. He just stood there, like a deer caught in a poacher's headlight, not believing Daniel actually found the courage to hit him, and in public.

"Saul," said Daniel, upon the realization he had stunned Saul. "You ain't hearing me, brother. These kids were playing here first, so we should leave them alone and let them play. It's only fair. Sure, you're king of the hill in this neighborhood, everybody knows it, but these kids look up to you—us. We have to set an example. Don't you want them to know you understand what it was like being a kid? Always being picked on by some hardheaded bully; knowing there was nothing you could do about it? Huh? Don't you remember those days?"

"I ain't never been bullied."

"Then try to remember how it was for me; your having to take up for me all the time."

Saul chuckle, remembering the times he had to come to Daniel's rescue. He looked over at the boy he had taken the ball from and glared angrily, because the boy was smirking. Saul knew it was only because Daniel had punched him. He rubbed his jaw and worked it back and forth. When Daniel saw him do that, he said, "Sorry 'bout that, but I needed to get your attention. We're friends, or at least we use to be, so I'm hoping you don't take that punch too personally."

Saul looked pass Daniel, toward the older crowd. He beckoned for one of the guys to throw him the ball. When he caught it, Saul handed it over to Daniel.

"We'd better win," he said and walked toward the goal on the other side of the court, away from the children.

Relieved, Daniel sighed. He bounced the ball several times, and while walking to the other side of the court, watched the other players jockey for position. To start the game, Daniel raised the ball up over his head, and threw it to Saul. Then charging forward, Daniel ran up to Saul to create a post. Saul took advantaged of the move. He turned and leaped into the air; taking the shot, but it didn't go into the basket. Instead, it hit the rim and bounced up. When Daniel saw the ball, he leaped and caught it in midair, and then slammed it into the basket.

"Aaagghh!" he crowed.

"Now, that's what I'm talking 'bout!" shouted Saul. He ran back to mid-court and called for the ball.

When Daniel darted toward the goal, from the side of the court, Saul, recognized the *alley-oop* move, and lobbed the ball into the air. Daniel caught it again and slammed it home. This time, when the ball went through the net-less rim, it ricocheted off someone's head and rolled out into the grass.

"GET THE BALL!" yelled someone.

"GET THE BALL!" repeated the voice in Daniel's daydream. Startled, he raised his hands and caught the basketball, just as it was about to hit him in the face.

"Whoa!" exclaimed Daniel, "that was an adrenaline rush!"

Daniel looked at the ball, and then toward the court. He saw an older, one-armed, man waving.

"Throw the ball, old man!" shouted the one-armed man.

Daniel threw the ball back and waited, until the game was over before walking up to the one-armed man.

"What's your name?"

"Bilbo..."

Bilbo did have two arms, although the smaller appendage was useless and had to be strapped down to his side, in order to prevent it from flopping around while the game was played.

"You got skills."

"Thanks," answered Bilbo as he wiped sweat from his face with a towel. After that, he draped the towel over his shoulder and unbuckled the belt securing his arm to his waist.

"I play, so these boys can see there are no excuses in life. Guess it's just my way of giving back to the community, know what I mean?"

"Yeah…I'm feeling you," answered Daniel, but then he asked, "Do you know a dude name Solomon?"

"You mean Saul, don't you?" replied Bilbo, and because of the way he spat out the name, it was obvious Bilbo didn't care for Saul.

"Yeah, Saul…Seen 'em around here lately?"

Bilbo glanced back over his shoulder, to make sure no one was paying attention. When he faced Daniel again he asked, "You a cop?"

Daniel pulled back his coat and flashed the badge clipped to his belt.

"Walk with me," he said and they walked away from the court.

"My name is Detective Daniel Rose, maybe you heard of me?"

"What makes you think that?"

"Cause I grew up around here. In fact, I still own my mother's house down on Pueblo Drive. Saul and I used to hang together, back in the day."

"If you were one of Saul's boys, then how come you don't know where he is? And how's it you turned out to be a cop, while he still lives on the dark side?"

"It's a long story, but needless to say, I need to know if he's back in town. Is he?"

"Yeah, but I'm doing everything I can to stay away from him. He's bad news. How in the hell you think I got this way?"

Bilbo grabbed his limp arm by the wrist and held it up, so Daniel could get a better look at it.

"He did that, huh?"

Bilbo nodded.

"Yeah…Fifteen years ago."

"How'd it happen?"

"We were playing flag football…right here, in this park, when Saul showed up and said he wanted to play. No one wanted to play with him, because we all knew he liked to cheat. And it didn't matter we were playing flag football, he tackled everyone. I was able to evade him, for most of the game, but that only pissed him off…"

# # #

While skillfully weaving passed Saul's team, Bilbo made one fatal mistake. Once, when he crossed the goal line, he held the ball in the air and danced victoriously. When Saul saw him celebrating, he rushed forward and hurdled his massive body through the air, and landed on top of Bilbo.

"How's that feel, speedy?" Saul punctuated his question with an elbow to Bilbo's back, prompting Bilbo to cry, "Argh!"

"Saul, that's enough," yelled one of the other plays, as they ran over to help Bilbo.

"Com'on man, it's just a game!" another shouted.

Saul rose off Bilbo, and standing over him triumphantly, refused to let anyone help, until he spotted the football Bilbo had dropped. Saul picked it up and dropped down to one knee.

"He fumbled, so that's a touch back!"

The other players, including Saul's own teammates, ignored the victory chant. They rushed to Bilbo and rolled him onto his back. Bilbo screamed again, but this time it sounded painful. Someone yelled for an ambulance, but another person suggested loading him into his car; saying he could get Bilbo to the hospital faster.

#

"So they picked me up and drove me to the hospital," continued Bilbo, "My arm was broken in several places, and I had a pinched nerve too. That's what paralyzed my arm. They should've never moved me."

"That sucks," said Daniel, but then he asked, "So...Is Saul back in town?"

"Yeah...I saw him a few weeks ago."

"Where...around here?"

"I ran into him at the Promenade Bar over in Buckhead. He was decked out and looking all gangsta'. There was a drop dead, fine high yella' sis'ta hanging off his arm too."

"Can you describe her? I mean, would you know her if you saw her again?"

"S'pose so," answered Bilbo, so Daniel reached into his coat pocket and pulled out a picture of Terrie. When he held it up Bilbo said, "Yeah, that's her. She was all over him."

"Anything else?" asked Daniel, obviously disappointed Terrie had decided to go out with Saul after all.

"Well, there was a white boy sitting with him too. He looked familiar, but I couldn't put a finger on where I knew 'em from. He was sporting a cute little black chick too."

"What did you do after that?"

"Hell, I was having a good time, 'til I saw Saul. After that, I downed my beer and got the hell out'ta that place. I figured it was only a matter of time 'fo a fight started over them bitches."

"Guess I don't blame you."

Daniel pulled out his notepad and jotted down Bilbo's comments, and his thoughts.

"What date was that?" he asked, and Bilbo said, "I don't remember…a couple of weeks ago? Look…"

Bilbo cast a quick glance back over his shoulder and saw the boys watching him, and Daniel.

"Man…I got'ta go, or else they'll think I'm snitching."

"Oh, all right."

Daniel looked around, at the boys, and then said, "Anything I can do to make this right, so you won't have any problems?"

"Yeah…Pop me upside the head and say you want your money by next week. And say it loudly, so they can hear. They know I gamble."

"Okay," replied Daniel, and then, without warning, he slapped Bilbo and pushed him to the ground.

"Don't make me come looking for you!"

Bilbo scrambled back. He tried to get up, but Daniel booted him in the butt, and without looking back, walked away.

When the boys saw what was happening to Bilbo, they rushed to his aid.

"You all right?" one of them asks, while helping Bilbo to his feet.

"Who was that fucker?" another asked. He reached into his pocket and pulled out a pistol. "Want me to smoke that son-of-a-bitch?"

Bilbo reached out and placed his hand on the gun, and he gently forced the boy to lower it.

"That's my bookie…He's owed money, so it's all good."

"Okay, but he needs to recognize…We don't play that shit 'round this hood. We watch out for our own."

"True that!" exclaimed another boy, loud enough for Daniel to hear.

#

27

The screams made Jeremy scrambled from beneath the trailer. He ran toward the sounds blindly and stumbled and fell several times, until he saw the girls. When he approached, one of them raised her head and looked directly at Jeremy. Her mouth opened, and she tried to screamed, but the only sound emerging from her mouth were gurgles. She grabbed hold of the forklift blade and tried to extricate herself. When Jeremy saw what she was trying to do, he grabbed the girl's hand and pulled her. The girl yanked her hand, free of Jeremy's grasp, and began to flail wildly. Her head fell backwards and blood sprayed from the wound in her neck.

"Ugh!" cried Jeremy, revolted by the smell of the warm blood. He backed away, and was just about to leave, when the girl began to weep.

"Don't cry, pretty lady."

Jeremy approached the girl. He reached out to touch her, but she recoiled backwards.

"I'm wanna help, but I don't know what to do."

After a moment of intense thinking, Jeremy snapped his fingers. He had come up with an idea.

"I know! I can lower the blades, and when your feet touch the ground, maybe you can try to run away. Let's do that and see what happens then."

Jeremy walked around, and was about to climbed on the forklift, but he accidently grabbed hold of one of the levers and the vehicle's *blades began to rise. The girl's body stiffened, but then slumped over; she was dead.*

# # #

Jeremy's dreams were becoming more and more intense, and they seemed real to him. When he sat up this morning, Jeremy wondered if it was because of the drugs, or was he simply loosing his mind?

When he looked down at his clothes, Jeremy saw blood spattered all over his shirt. *What have I done?* He wondered. Looking around, Jeremy sees a pair of eyes. They're in the furthest corner of his car, and they're staring out at him.

"Roscoe, Is that you?" he asked, nervously.

"Who else would it be? What, you think just because you sleep, I'd go away…huh?"

The ghostly dog lumbered forward, and sat back on its haunches in front of Jeremy. Raising one hind leg, it struggled to keep its head in place, while it licked itself.

"Shesh, I'm glad it's you."

Jeremy ran his hands through his wooly hair. He felt something wet and sticky, so he raised them up and held them in the ambient light coming into the car through the newspaper covered windows. He sighed, because they were clean.

It was a dream, he thought and looked up at the dog.

"I had one hell of a dream."

The dog dropped its leg, and looking curiously at Jeremy, it said, *"You had one hell of a night too."*

"What's that s'pose to mean?"

"Don't you remember?"

"What are you talking about? What I do?"

"Never mind, what's the use?"

Jeremy remembered his dream, and the girls, but he didn't say anything about it. He just wanted to forget. He slid over to the car door and pushed it open. After he got out, Jeremy discovered his home had been tagged again.

"You'd think they'd get tired of doing this, wouldn't you?"

"If you'd let me, I could teach them a lesson in humility. I could scare the hell out of 'em."

Roscoe jumped out of the car.

"No, that wouldn't work. The best thing to do is go and talk to their parents. Tell them what's going on, that should work."

"And how do you expect to find their parents? Hell you don't even know who they are."

"I'll just go knock on some doors in the neighborhood; bound to find them that way."

"Sure…that'll work."

Roscoe walked over to the loveseat and lies on his back, with his legs splayed open, so the morning sunshine could warm his underbelly.

"I'm gonna lie here, and soak up some sun. You go on…knock on them doors. Let me know how that goes for you."

"You're just gonna let me do this all alone?"

"Yep…being that it's your idea, I figure you should handle it by yourself."

"Sorry fucker," mumbled Jeremy, as he walked pass the loveseat and out of his campsite.

28

In the beginning, Louise's marriage to Daniel was no different than any other. It was passionate and very, very, intimate and they could talk about anything, including details of cases Daniel wasn't supposed to discuss. Particularly, those the media didn't bother to report; other than the obits for the unfortunate women and children who found themselves on the wrong side of a beating.

The problems Daniel and Louise experienced manifested slowly, and over time. Eventually, Louise found herself physically and emotionally isolated from the man of her dreams. She knew being a cop's wife meant having to spend some time alone. After all, she is the daughter of a Captain and knows what stress signs to look for in her husband.

Louise knew the violence Daniel had witnessed was taking its toll on him; both mentally and physically. His nightmares were becoming more and more lucid, and they kept him awake during the night. Even when Daniel did manage to fall asleep, he cried and mumbled the names of the victims he couldn't save.

Mornings in the Rose home were typically quiet, but today, this morning is different. Louise's real estate business was picking up, and she was excited about the appointment she had scheduled today.

"I've been playing phone tag with this guy from Los Angeles for several weeks now," she said to Daniel, while they sat at the breakfast table. "His last message said he would be in town today, and that he wanted to meet, so we can discuss my being the primary agent for the subdivisions he's building in and around Atlanta. Isn't that great?"

Daniel raised his head, from the coffee cup he had been quietly staring down into, and looked at Louise. She was happy, that much was obvious, but Daniel had too many unpleasant things rattling around in his mind to care.

"I dreamt about the little boy last night," he mumbled, putting a damper on Louise's good news. "He was standing in front of me shouting and flailing his arms, as if he was trying to warn me about something."

"Really?" asked Louise. The joy she felt quickly drained away, and it showed on her face.

Daniel pursed his lips and tried to smile, but it was weak. He leaned forward and blew over the top of his coffee, and then took a sip.

"So…what's the plan today? You gonna seal the deal with this guy? Make a million bucks, so I can retire?"

"Yeah, I'm gonna seal the deal all right."

Louise pushed back, angrily from the table, and stands. She faces the stove and picks up a kettle of boiling water. The water is poured into a travel mug that has a tea bag in it. Louise dips the bag in the water several times, until a light brew of tea formed. She threw the used tea bag into the waste basket, and then screwed the top onto her mug. After picking up her keys, along with her briefcase, and the mug, Louise stormed toward the door.

"What…no kiss?" asked Daniel, when Louise walked away. He was resting his elbows on the table, holding the cup up to his mouth; about to take another sip.

"I tried to kiss you this morning, but you didn't seem too interested." Louise paused at the door and looked back. "In fact, I've tried to make love to you several times, over the past several weeks, but you blew me off. So why would I allow you to kiss me now? Huh…Detective Rose?"

After Louise exited the kitchen, and went into the garage, Daniel rose from his seat and followed her. He rushed up behind Louise, and as unromantically as he could, wrapped his arms around her waist.

"Daniel, stop it!" squealed Louis, but Daniel ignoring her protest, humped suggestively against her backside.

"When you get home, I'm gonna rock your world."

While groping Louise's butt, Daniel felt something odd, so he hiked up her skirt

"What the hell's going on?"

Louise wasn't wearing any underwear, just stockings and a garter belt.

"Why aren't you wearing any underwear?"

Louise snatched her dress down, and without taking her eyes off Daniel, she raised her hand and pointed the remote at the garage door.

"What's it to you?" she asked as the garage door began to rise. "You've never been interested in what I wear before, so why's today different?"

"B-But—," stammered Daniel, but because he didn't have an answer, he closed his mouth.

"You're just interested in dead bodies, not hot ones like mine. Or could it be you've grown so accustomed to seeing that little boy in your dreams that now you're craving little boys? Huh, Detective Rose?"

Daniel steeled his emotions, while listening to Louise's uncharacteristic attack on his person.

God, not again, he thought, believing he had alienated yet another wife.

"Okay," he replied softly, stepping away from the car. "Go on to work. We'll discuss this later...when we've both settled down a bit. Okay?"

Louise got into her car, cranked its engine, and slammed the gear shift into reverse. When she floored the gas pedal the rear wheels squealed as she backed out into the street.

#

Several blocks away, while sitting at a red light, Louise gripped her steering wheel tightly. After taking several relaxing deep breaths, she reached for her cell phone.

What am I doing? She wondered while dialing the number of the man she had hoped was going to change her fate.

"Hello…Mr. Thompson?" she asks, sounding more like an infatuated school girl, instead of an aspiring real estate baron.

"Hey, sweetheart…What are you doing up so early?"

"Early? It's nearly nine in the morning here in Atlanta."

"Well…it's four in the morning here. Did you forget about the time difference?"

"No…I didn't," answered Louise, "I just needed someone to talk to. My man and I…Well…we had an argument this morning and—"

Louise stopped speaking suddenly. *What are you doing girl?* She asked herself, but for reasons Louise couldn't begin to explain, she kept talking.

"—I just needed someone to talk to."

"I understand," replied Saul, pretending to care. "I tell you what…" Saul's voice perked up, "I'll wake up my pilot, so we can leave early. Okay? I mean, if we leave within the hour, we should arrive in Atlanta sometime around noon. We can meet in my hotel lobby and have lunch."

"Really…? You can do that?"

"Com'on, I own the jet."

"Oh, I forgot!" replied Louise, feeling silly. "Will you call me when you land?"

"You know I will…bye now!"

Louise held the dead cell phone against her ear and daydreamed about Saul; who he was and what he looked like. But when the sound of honking horns brought her back to reality, she looked up. The traffic light had turned green, a long time ago, and was about to turn red again.

"Okay! Okay! I'm going!"

#

After flipping his cell phone shut, Saul dropped it on the night stand next to his bed. He laid his head back on his pillow and smiled; pleased with himself.

"Think she suspects anything?"

Tim was lying in the bed with Saul. He was on the other side of it, grinding slowly against the body of the young female decorator he had picked up from the convention center. Her mouth was duct taped shut, but that was unnecessary now, because the girl wasn't going to scream. She was in shock.

"Naw," answered Saul. "She bought my lie, hook, line and sinker. Her daddy maybe a captain, and her husband a detective, but she's one dumb naïve bitch; thinks she's gonna make a killing, selling real estate."

Tim laughed. He grunted and releasing himself, ejaculated into the cavity of the young decorator. When he withdrew, he rolled over on to his back, while at the same time, pushed the girl toward Saul.

"She's all yours now."

Saul grabbed the girl by her hair and pulled her head back. He flicked the knife so quickly across her throat; she didn't feel a thing as the blade opened it up.

"Dumb bitch…"

# # #

29

At the Peachtree Plaza Hotel's Sun Dial Restaurant, Louise is greeted by a handsome black man, who she thought was a waiter.

"Hi, I'm meeting someone…Solomon Thompson."

The black man smiled, and flashing his perfect white teeth, he held out his hand, but Louise refused it.

"Please," he said, "Call me Saul."

Louise held her hand against her mouth, but the expression on her face said it all. She was embarrassed.

"I'm sorry, but…I thought you were a waiter."

Quickly extending her hand, Louise placed it inside Saul's massive paw. He raised it to his lips and gave it a sensual kiss.

"Don't apologize. I get that all the time," Saul led Louise to their table. "I hope you're hungry, because I am. Ain't had southern cooking in quite a while. It's hard to get in L.A."

"I guess I could eat a bite," replied Louise as she took her seat.

After Saul sat, he hailed the *real* waiter. While Louise ordered, Saul stared down at his menu, and didn't see the uniformed officer walk up to their table.

"Don't I know you?" he asked, and when Saul heard him, he looked up; startled. He gulped, and tried to remember where he had met the policeman, but before he could say anything, Louise leaped up from her seat and embraced the policeman.

"Daddy!" she squealed, sounding like a little girl.

"Baby girl, what are you up to today?"

While hugging Louise, Darryl stared at Saul. He had raised the menu higher, deliberately concealing his face.

"And who is this?" asked Darryl, but Saul kept looking down at the Menu.

Pretending he had finally decided what it was he wanted, Saul pointed at the menu and the waiter acknowledged his choice with a nod, and then walked away.

When Saul looked up from the menu, and looked at Darryl, he stood and extended his hand.

"My name is Solomon Thompson, sir." Saul glanced at Louise and smiled. "Your daughter has convinced me she can sell matches to people in hell, so I've asked her to consider managing the sales of the homes my firm is planning to build here in Atlanta."

"Really?" asked Darryl, but after releasing Saul's hand, and continuing with the conversation, he pulled out a handkerchief and wiped the moisture from his palm. Saul was sweating.

"And where's that?" he asked, and Saul seemed to be put off by the question.

"I beg your pardon?"

"I asked, 'where are you building?' I know this city like the back of my hand, so where?"

Saul hesitated. He had not expected to be grilled by a detective's captain.

"Our first site is in the Camp Creek corridor," he replied, finally. "There's a track of prime real estate bordering it; Red Oaks...you know it?"

"Yeah, but that's deep in the *'hood'*...your firm knows that, don't they?"

"It won't be the hood after we're done with it. All of our houses will be upscale, and their minimum cost will be around three hundred thousand. It'll be the black *Buckhead*."

Saul was referring to the ritzy downtown Atlanta neighborhood, where only the rich and famous lived.

Darryl's suspicious eyes moved from Saul to Louise. When she signaled for him to leave, Darryl smiled. Realizing he was intruding, he excused himself and said, "Well, I got to go. Be good."

"I will daddy," answered Louise, but when she looked across the table at Saul, she flashed him a mischievous smile.

"Don't worry sir; I won't let her get into any trouble."

Darryl acknowledged Saul's comment with a polite smile, and then he turned and walked away.

While taking his seat, Saul kept staring at Darryl, until the captain took his place among a group of well heeled business men on the other side of the room.

"Look," he said to Louise, "Why don't we finish this meeting in my room? I can have the waiter send up the meal."

"I don't know…"

While mulling over the idea, Louise looked across the room and saw her father. He was glaring angrily at her.

"Okay," she blurted suddenly, when she turned to Saul. "Sure…why not?"

"Okay? Good!"

Saul grabbed the first waiter walking by, and handed him a twenty dollar bill.

"Have our meals brought up to my room."

"Okay sir," said the waiter, while looking down at the crumpled twenty. "I'll let *your* waiter know to do that."

#

Once they were in his room, Saul plopped down on his bed. Louise sat in the seat located in the corner across from it. They talked about business for a while, but eventually their voices fell silent. When Louise began to speak again, she talked about her husband, and at some point during the conversation, she disclosed the fact they had not made love in months. And because of that revelation, she began to weep.

"Don't cry."

Saul moved over to Louise, and placed an arm around her shoulders.

"I'm sure this'll all work itself out in due time," he said, "A fine thing like your self...I know he won't hold out much longer. Hell, if you were mine, I'd fuck—uh...I mean, I'd make love to you every night."

Louise looked into Saul's face and stared into his dreamy eyes.

"That's all right," she said, smiling. "I like to fuck too."

Believing Louise had opened the door; Saul stood, and holding her hand, led Louise back over to the bed.

"I didn't say *we* were going to fuck," she said, but never stopped walking. And when they got to the bed, she crawled up onto it without being prompted.

Saul climbed on the bed too, and after crawling next to Louise, his mouth met hers. He had expected her to resist, and was prepared for that, but she didn't. Instead, Louise opened her mouth and welcomed his probing tongue.

Saul rubbed his hand across Louise's leg, and because she didn't resist that either, he moved his hand under her dress and touched her pubic hair.

"You don't have any underwear on."

"Because you've offered me a great opportunity, I hadn't planned on leaving without a deal; no matter the cost. This could put my name on the map."

Saul grinned wolfishly, and then buried his face against Louise's again. Using both of his hands, Saul grabbed Louise by her ankles and pulled her legs up.

"Oh gawd!" she cried, "It's been so long, I forgot what it felt like."

After experiencing an orgasm, Louise unlocked her legs and pushed Saul away. She curled up into a fetal position and began to cry. Saul tried to comfort her, but Louise was inconsolable.

"What have I done?" she cried, and then scrambling off the bed, Louise grabbed her purse and rushed out of the room.

"Wait!" shouted Saul, but the door slammed shut before he could say another word.

"Damn!" he groaned, and then said, "You can come out now."

When the bathroom door opened, Tim walked out. He was naked and excited, but when he saw the empty room, he turned to Saul.

"What the hell happened?"

"I don't know," replied Saul with a shrug. "One minute she was all into it, and then the next, she's running out the door, crying hysterically."

"Shit...and I done already took that Viagra pill! What am I gonna do now, huh? I can't leave the room like this."

Tim stared down at his pharmaceutically enhanced pecker, and then up at Saul, pleading.

"Don't worry." Saul crossed the room and dropped down to his knees in front of Tim. "I'll take care of that for you."

###

30

The Claremont hotel was a dump; a ten dollar a day flop house used only by hookers, dope feigns, and the occasional long haul truck driver.

The weekly housekeeper that discovered the body didn't speak English, and because she thought the police were there to deport her, she wouldn't even talk to them; despite the fact that one of them was Hispanic.

The only thing the manager could, or would, say about the men who rented the place was that they looked gay.

"Fags...I tell ya," he said, "Even though I try not to judge folk based on their sexual orientation."

I wonder why? Robney thought, but suspected it was because the hotel manager was a weirdo too. Half of his head was shaved, while the other side was covered with purple spikes of hair. The manager's ears had large o-rings in the lobes too, and tattoos cover both of his forearms. Robney suspected the tattoos converged somewhere on the man's chest, because of the one spiraling up his neck, like a parasitic vine.

"I'd like you to sit with one of our sketch artist. Think you can handle that?"

The manager shot a few quick glances around the parking lot to see if any of his tenants was watching. When he saw someone standing on the balcony, he shook his head.

"Look officer, I don't think I could be of much help. What I mean is; they were only in my office for a very short time."

"Yeah, but you *did* get a look at them...didn't you?"

Robney gestured for a uniformed policeman to come over.

"Take him in," he said, "If he refuses to help, arrest him for obstruction."

Robney faced the manager again and added, "Either way, you're going to tell me what I need to know."

"But—," the manager protested, "—I don't know anything!"

Ignoring the weirdo's protest, Robney walked back to the hotel room, where he stood in the open doorway and watched Becky. He pulled out a handkerchief and covered his mouth and nose.

"This looks familiar, doesn't it?" he asks, speaking through the cloth.

"Yeah...," answered Becky, when she glanced over her shoulder and saw Robney in the doorway. "...right down to the rose on the floor."

"Guess I need to have that talk with Detective Rose, after all...huh?"

Becky doesn't answer, because she knew Robney knew what he had to do without her telling him. She raised the camera she was holding and snapped several pictures of the body.

"Okay—," she said, speaking to the coroner's assistants loitering outside the door. "She's all yours."

The two men, dressed in white jump suits, push their gurney pass Robney and effortlessly lifted the decomposing body off the bed. After placing it into the open body bag, on the gurney, they zipped it closed

Robney followed the coroner's assistants out of the room and watched, while they loaded the gurney into their van. Once the van's doors were closed, he strolled over to next hotel room and knocked on the door.

"What the hell you want!?" growled the old fat man that cracked the door. He was wearing only boxer shorts and appeared to have been asleep.

Robney held up his badge, and the fat man, thinking the hotel was being raided, slammed the door shut.

"He's rabbiting!" yelled Robney, and he quickly tells one of the policemen to run around the back of the hotel.

After kicking the door open, Robney saw the underage girl lying in the bed. She was naked, and at first, Robney thought she was drunk and had passed out, because of all of the empty liquor bottles on the table. So he walked pass the bed and too the bathroom, where the fat man had ran.

"Hey!" he yelled through the closed door, "Get'cho fat ass out here…now!"

While standing outside the locked bathroom door, waiting, Robney hears sounds; crying and grunting, so thinking someone was being held in the room by the fat man, he backed away, and then kicked open the door.

The fat man, trying to escape, had tried to climb out of the small window in the bathroom and had gotten himself stuck.

"You fat fuck," sighed Robney, relieved no one else was in trouble. He holstered his revolver and said, "Get down from that window."

"I can't," replied the fat man, sounding embarrassed. "I'm stuck."

"Serves you right…" Robney grabbed the radio clipped to his belt. "We're going to need the fire department dispatched to my 10-20."

"Copy that," replied a feminine voice.

"Arrest him too—" Robney tells the other officers entering the hotel room. "—after he's extracted from that window."

"What's the charge?" one asked.

"Being a fat fuck?" chuckles another.

Robney chuckled too, until he walked over to the bed to wake up the girl.

"No…with murder," he said, "she's dead."

"What'chu mean, dead?" shouted the fat man from the window. "We just got here a few moments ago! Hell, I ain't even fucked her yet?"

"But you had enough time to cram all of this booze down her throat, huh?"

Robney walked back into the bathroom, and angrily grabbed the fat man by his feet. Deciding not to wait for the firemen, he yanked on the feet, until the fat man came free and fell into the bathtub beneath the window.

"Hey!" cried the fat man as he scrambled over and sat up, "That's police brutality!"

"Get your fat ass up!"

Robney grabbed the fat man by his hair and pulled him up to his feet. Then, despite the man's protest, the other policemen handcuffed him and lead him out of the room, to one of the waiting patrol cars.

"What the hell happened here?" asked Becky, when she walked into the room to see what all of the commotion was about.

"We got another Vic," answered Robney, pointing to the girl in the bed.

"And you think that man is the doer?"

"Yeah, so compare this crime scene with the one next door and tell me I'm right, so I can close this case."

Becky scoured the room with her trained eyes, and then quickly says, "This guy didn't kill the girl next door."

"Are you sure? Don't be too hasty here. Take a closer look at the body."

"Okay, if you insist."

"I insist..." replied Robney, so Becky walked over to the bed and pulled back the bed covers.

The first thing Becky observes is the sores and bruises covering the girl's torso; someone had enjoyed beating her, but that was some time back, because none of the injuries were fresh. When she raised the girl's arm, Becky spots needle tracks; some are still oozing blood.

"Based on what I'm seeing here," she says, "This young lady shot up recently...maybe less than a half hour ago. She wasn't killed by the same person who killed that girl next door, because she wasn't slit open like a slaughtered hog. Odds are, she OD'd, which leads me to believe that poor slob, that you're trying to pin this on, is probably telling the truth."

"Okay, but he was trying to get his freak on with a minor, and that *is* still illegal in this state, ain't it?"

"Yes, it is." Becky replied, agreeing the fat man had committed a crime, but then she adds, "I'll photo document this room too and gather up what evidence I can find, but you'll have to wait for the coroner to rule on the exact cause of death. Right now, my preliminary findings are that this was a simple case of accidental drug over-dose. Okay?"

"Okay, whatever…" answered Robney, and he stormed out of the room.

# # #

31

While driving around the old neighborhood, looking for Saul, Daniel couldn't help but to wonder what Louise meant; when she said what she said earlier that morning.

What did she mean; I never pay attention to what she wears? And why would she go to a meeting wearing no underwear? Have I been that neglectful?

A blue Avenger ran a traffic light, and nearly hit Daniel's car. When he saw the driver, Daniel thought it was Saul, so he turned the corner, and followed it. His first instinct was to flash his lights, and pull over the vehicle, but the radio distracts Daniel.

"Detective Rose, Captain Peterson is requesting you to return to the station."

"Can it wait? I'm on a stake out."

"No. He said, and I quote, 'Pronto!'"

"Shit," groaned Daniel, and then, without signaling, he executes a u-turned in front of the on-coming traffic.

When Saul and Tim heard the squeal of tires, followed by the sound of multiple horns, Tim turns around in his seat and looks back. When he spots Daniel's car, speeding in the opposite direction, he said, "That was a copper, wasn't it?"

Saul glanced up into his rear-view mirror and stares at the car.

"Yeah, he's been tailing us since we came through that last intersection; probably ran the plates too. But this car ain't stolen, so he probably went off to arrest some other thieving sap. Told'ja it was better to rent a car, instead of stealing one."

"Guess you are smarter than you look." Tim turned around and faced forward. "What's our next step?"

"I'm gonna have to call Louise again and apologize. And see if she's willing to meet me again, so we can move forward with our real estate deal."

"Then what…?"

"I think we need to quit fucking 'round, and go on and get her. Take her to a place no one would expect, especially Daniel."

"Where's that?"

"A place that's right under his nose."

"What about me boy…Darryl? He saw you and her together…won't he connect the dots?"

"He won't have to, 'cause we're gonna call 'em, and tell 'em what we're doing to his little girl. Ain't that what you want?"

"Uh-huh," Tim replies, with a slow nod of his head. He clinched his fist and cracked his knuckles. "That fucker's got'ta pay for what he took from me."

"Yeah, they both are gonna pay."

# # #

32

Daniel stepped off of the elevator and immediately saw Robney, and Captain Peterson, going through his desk.

"Is there something I can help you find?" he asked as he approached them. "I mean, I could give you my laptop and password, if that'll help."

Darryl looked up. Embarrassed, he knows he should have waited for Daniel, but Robney didn't care. He enjoyed prying into Daniel's business.

"Yeah, that'll work…" he said when he looked up and saw Daniel. "So we can see what else you've been hiding."

"HEY FUCK YOU!"

Daniel walked up to Robney, and while staring him in the face, addressed Darryl.

"Captain, just what the hell's going on?"

Captain Peterson didn't answer, but instead, turned and walked toward his office.

"I want both of you in my office…now!" he growled angrily. "We need to cross reference your cases."

"What? Why?"

Daniel moved around to the back of his desk, to check and see if anything was missing or out of place. When he pulled open his 'old case' file drawer and saw all of his files were gone, Daniel stood and spoke to Darryl's retreating backside.

"None of those cons are connected to any of my active cases, or Robney's. I just keep them for references."

"Yeah...sure," said Robney, "Then tell me, what about your relationship to the victims, huh? What about that?"

"I...uh—captain..." Daniel took his eyes off of Darryl's backside and looked at Robney. "I don't have to answer to this twit, do I?"

Captain Peterson stopped, just outside his office, and looked back. He knew; if he continued to allow their discussion to remain public, it would create a schism in the squad room and people would take sides.

"In my office...NOW!" he commanded, and then, speaking directly to Daniel, said, "Bring your high yellow ass in here!"

Daniel slammed the drawer loudly and then walked angrily passed Robney.

"Fuck'n wop," he mumbled, and Robney replied with, "Coon..."

When the captain heard the exchange he shouted, "Cut that crap out! What the hell y'all think this is...a playground?"

#

After Daniel and Robney walked into the captain's office, Captain Peterson closed the blinds in his windows, so no one could see or read their body language. When he finished, he turned and moved to the other side of his desk and took his seat.

"Sit down, both of you."

The detectives sat.

"After the last shouting match you two had the other day; I pulled your personnel files, and it seems you were quite a pair in the academy; best friends, until your last year."

"Yeah, so?" answered both detectives.

"So...? So what happened to make you such rivals? You're both good detectives, and I'd hate to have to transfer either one of you."

Robney and Daniel glanced at each other. When they looked back at the captain, and spoke, they did so at the same time.

"He took advantage of his color, which is why he scored higher than me," said Robney.

"Captain, he's just jealous, because I'm smarter."

Darryl chuckled, and snorted. He placed both hands, palm down, on his desk and leaned forward.

"You two are idiots, you know that? We've got, what appears to be, a serial killer stalking our city, and you're squabbling like first graders fighting over crayons."

"But captain!" each detective blurted. "He started it!" The detectives pointed at each other.

"Damn," Daniel groaned, when he realized he didn't really know why he hated Robney.

"Christ," Robney moaned, because when he thought about it, he could not remember why he hated Daniel either.

Both men stood and faced each other. Robney extended his hand and said, "Brother, I've been a *real* jerk, haven't I?"

"Yes you have—" replied Daniel, but before Robney could react to him, Darryl said, "Detective…"

Daniel glanced at Darryl, and taking the hint, accepts Robney's hand.

"—but so have I," he adds. "And I have missed our friendship."

"Me too!" replied Robney, with a broad grin. He pulled Daniel forward and they both hugged each other, as if they hadn't seen each other for years.

"Okay, now I'm gonna be sick," said the captain. He picked up one of the files on his desk and began to review it. "So now, can we get back to business?"

The detectives sat and pulled out their note books, but before they start, Daniel confessed about his past relationships with the victims. He was quickly ruled out as a suspect, although they all agreed he was the connecting fiber in the case.

"Are you sure you've checked all of your old cases?" asked Robney. "There's got to be someone you know who could be responsible for these murders?"

"I've checked out everyone I've arrested. They're either dead, still in prison, or have gone completely straight."

"What about the humps that got off? Maybe you roughed up someone who's still pissed off?"

"I don't know…" answered Daniel, mulling over the question. He rubbed his temples. "I don't keep track of *everyone* I've encountered, do you?"

"No…I don't," replied Robney, understanding.

Darryl had been staring down at the crime pictures throughout the discussion. When he looked up from them, he pointed to the roses.

"This rose, it has to be referring to you, Daniel. This fucker *is* targeting you and he wants you to know it."

"That's what I thought after I saw the second rose, but I couldn't make the connection."

"How's he choosing the Vic's?" asked Robney, and then, suddenly, they all had an epiphany.

"Because he knows them too!" they exclaimed.

Daniel whipped out his laptop and went directly to the internet, where he typed in *'Central High School Alumni'*.

"What are you looking for?" asked Darryl, and Daniel said, "This asshole knows who I know…that's how he's choosing his targets, which means he's got to be someone from my childhood; someone who's holding a grudge from way back. I just don't know who, or why?"

When pictures of his old classmates began to populate the screen, Daniel doesn't recognize many of them.

"Wow! We were so young back then," he mumbled, once he saw his own senior photo.

"Yeah, but even psychopaths were young once." Robney was staring down at the pictures on the screen. "They just hadn't figured out a way to kill and get away with it yet."

"Does anyone jump out as our doer?" he asked, and Daniel shook his head.

"Naw, not yet but…WAIT!" Daniel pointed at Saul's picture. "Him I know! We were best friends, until he did a couple of questionable things I didn't approve of, so we went our separate ways."

"Think back, was he…you know, crazy?"

Daniel stared at the screen and slowly nods. When he looked up, at the captain, he said, "Yeah. Come to think of it, he was out there. You know the type, a bully…forcing himself on the girls."

"He ever charged with anything as a juvenile?" asked Robney, but before Daniel could answer, someone knocked on the captain's door. It was the department's sketch artist.

"Enter..."

"Excuse me captain, but I've finished with the witness and..." The sketch artist held up two drawings. "Here's what he says the two men looked like."

When Daniel saw the first drawing, he instantly recognized Saul's face, but not the other.

"Him I know, but I don't recognize the other man."

"I do," answered Captain Peterson, so Daniel turned from the drawing and looked back at Darryl. There's concern on his face.

"Who is he?"

"My old friend, Tim Kelso..." answered Darryl, "I testified for the prosecution during his trial, and he got the max; ten years. He nearly killed a girl."

Daniel moved the curser on his laptop, and accessing the department's intranet, opens Saul's and Tim's files.

"Saul was convicted of rape and given ten years, but because of the over crowding in California, he was shipped to Taft Federal prison, where he served his time."

When Daniel changed the screen, it displayed Tim's file, and what he saw was disturbing.

"Captain, it seems your friend was sent to Taft too and his cellmate was Solomon Thompson...a.k.a. Saul."

"When was their release dates?" asked Robney, so Daniel moved the curser again and changed the screen.

"Tim; nearly a year ago, but Saul was released only five months ago. Tim is free and clear, but Saul is still on parole. His P.O. is Jeff Oliver."

"Okay, you two...go pay Mr. Oliver a visit. Find out where his boy is. We've got to get these two humps off of the street, before they kill someone else."

"Huh...both of us?" asked Robney, curiously.

"Yeah," answered Darryl. "Because...now you're partners."

"But captain, I work better on my own. You know that," said Robney, with an unapologetic glance toward Daniel. "No offense Bro..."

"None taken," replied Daniel, "Because I work better alone too and besides, you'd stand out like a sore thumb in the neighborhoods I frequent."

"Squash that shit!" barked Darryl, "just go out and find that son-of-a-bitch, will you!"

Daniel faced the captain, and noticing the tears streaming down his face, asked, "What's wrong? You're not concerned about your old friend, are you?"

Darryl pointed a shaky finger at Saul's sketch.

"No," he answered, "I saw that mother fucker with my daughter earlier today. They were having lunch in the restaurant at the top of the Peachtree Hotel. I even talked to him; said he was building new subdivisions in the city. He even told me he wanted Louise to manage the sales for him."

"Oh God!" cried Daniel.

# # #

33

Louise sat in a warm bath and soaked; trying to wash away the sin she had committed in the name of business. Her phone vibrated, so she picked it up and stared at the caller's name. It was Saul. She tried to ignore the call, but Louise couldn't help but think about the money she could earn. So, after waiting a few moments, she pressed the green button.

"Hello…"

"Hey, are you okay?" asked Saul.

Louise's body reacts to Saul's sensuous voice; goose bumps rise on her arms and her nipples harden. She can even still feel the after affects of the orgasm she he while making love to Saul.

"Yes," she replied in a soft, submissive, tone.

"Look, let's just forget about this afternoon and move forward, okay?"

"You still want me to sell your houses?" asked Louise, and excited, she grabbed her towel and wiped her face.

"I mean—" she started to say, but Saul cut her off.

"Well, hell yeah!" he exclaimed. "Look…all bullshit aside, I think you're perfect for this project, and—"

Louise's phone vibrated again, so she pulled it back from her ear to see who was calling. When Louise saw Daniel's name flashing across the screen, she pushed the ignore button.

"—so what do you think?" is all Louise hears, when she returns the phone to her ear.

"I'm sorry, would you repeat that?"

"I've got to leave this evening," repeats Saul, "and was hoping we could meet up before I left. We can sign the contract I had my attorney draw up."

"What time?" asked Louise, while thrusting her fist silently into the air; celebrating.

"Let's say…around six? I've got to be in the air by seven, if I'm going to make the meeting with my investors in the morning."

"I don't want to meet in your room, if that's okay?"

Saul chuckled.

"Of course it's okay. My jet's housed at Charlie Brown Airport. Why don't we meet there; in the lobby of the Skylight Hotel? It ain't fancy, but it's convenient."

"Okay…I'll see you at six." Louise answers, and hangs up the phone.

#

The parole office lobby was nearly empty, when Daniel and Robney walked in. They strolled up to the receptionist, and flashing their badges, asked for Jeff Oliver.

"Do you have an appointment?" the male receptionist asked.

"No…but we need to speak with him anyway," answered Daniel, impatiently.

"Well…hold on. I'll see if he can see you."

"Look man, we're not one of your *clients*, so cut the bullshit and buzz us through."

Robney's hands were on the receptionist's desk. While leaning forward, and glaring down into the receptionist's face, he crumpled the sheets of paper that was scattered on it.

When the electronic lock buzzed, and Daniel and Robney walked through the door, they were greeted by a maze of cubicles.

"We're never gonna find him," moaned Daniel, which prompted Robney to shout, "LISTEN UP! WE'RE LOOKING FOR JEFF OLIVER! JEFF OLIVER!!"

Several heads popped up, but after seeing who had shouted, each of them sat back down.

When Jeff heard his name, he leaned out of the restroom and waved. Daniel pointed at the man and asked, "You Jeff Oliver?"

Jeff nods and holds up a finger, telling them to hold on a minute, because he's testing a parolee.

"Go sit on that bench and wait," Jeff said to the parolee, when they both walked out of the restroom. He was holding a cup of piss.

"It'll take a few minutes for the results," he said, speaking directly to the parolee. "I find you've been getting high again, I'm gonna revoke you. Understand?"

"But I swear…I ain't been doing anything," griped the man as he walked toward the bench.

"I don't know…" answered the parolee with a shrug. "I was drunk."

"Yeah, well…we'll see."

"Honest…Look, I found out my wife was fucking some other lump head and so, I got drunk and blew off some steam. It was either that, or I was gonna kill her…"

Jeff handcuffed the parolee to the bench. He stood over him and stared sympathetically at him for a moment, before walking away. When he looked at Daniel and Robney, Jeff held up the cup of piss and then gestured toward the nearest cubicle.

"Step into my office," he said, pointing to the cubicle. "I'll be there in a moment. I got'ta wash my hands."

"Take your time," said Daniel, but Robney pressed Jeff to hurry.

"We ain't got all day, you know!" he said loudly, while following Daniel into the small cubical.

When Jeff arrived, Robney complained about the receptionist's lack of protocol.

"Doesn't he know; when policemen come here, particularly detectives, we're here for a reason?"

"Don't be too harsh on him, he's new."

"What happened to the regular receptionist?" asked Daniel.

"She walked in on a burglar and was murdered."

"When was that?"

"Last week, Detective…what's this all about?"

"She didn't live off Bankhead, by any chance, did she?" asked Robney. He pulled out his note pad and flipped several pages, until he found what he was looking for. "…Glen Oaks?"

"Yeah, how'd you know?"

"Because…I'm the detective who discovered her body," answered Robney, and then he pulled out a mug shot of Saul and held it up. "Know him?"

Jeff groaned. Without being asked, he pulled open a drawer and grabbed Saul's file.

"During his first visit here, he and our original receptionist had a slight misunderstanding. It resulted in him being shackled to the bench in the hallway."

"What did he do?" asked Daniel, and Jeff looked up from the file.

"Actually, he didn't do anything. He just took an exception to the way she spoke to him; said it made him feel as though he was still in prison."

"Did he threaten her?" asked Robney. He was taking notes.

"No…Not that I'm aware of." Jeff handed the mug shot back to Robney. "What makes you think Saul murdered her?"

"We got a witness who puts him in the area the night your receptionist was killed," answered Daniel. "We need to talk to him. Do you know where he is; got an address or something?"

Jeff dropped his gaze and looked at the file again. When he looked up, he said, "125 Peachtree Street…downtown Atlanta."

"You're an idiot, you know that?" snapped Robney. He stood and pushed his chair back against the cubicle wall. The whole system shook and appeared as though the whole thing was going to collapse.

"He's an idiot," repeated Robney, while looking at Daniel. "This guy's an idiot."

"What's he talking about?" Jeff gazed curiously at the file again, wondering what he's missed. "What?"

"125 Peachtree Street is the Peachtree Plaza Hotel's address. Did you even *map search* the address on the internet to see if it was legit?"

"Why no, why would I?"

"Then what did you think; there was a flop house in down town Atlanta?"

"Hold on Rob," Daniel said, and he held up Tim's mug shot for Jeff to look at.

"Seen this guy? We think he and Saul have partnered up, and we think they're responsible for several murders around the city."

"You mean the Rose Murders, don't you?"

"Yeah…the Rose Murders," answered Daniel. "So…have you seen him, or not?"

"That's the guy that vouched for Saul a while back. Saul had this big idea about going into real estate. He proposed building some houses in the metro area, and this guy was backing him financially. The proposal he brought me was well written and well planned out, so I saw no reason for not letting him move forward with it. Did I do anything wrong?"

"No," answered Daniel, lowering the picture. "Do you know where we can find Tim Kelso?"

"Kelso…Kelso…" Jeff repeated the name. "Why does that name sound familiar?"

Daniel held up another picture, but his time it was an old mayoral campaign photo of Tim.

"Because the man in this picture, and that mug shot, is one and the same—Tim Kelso—Atlanta's former Mayor."

"You mean, the one sent to prison for corruption and rape?"

"Yeah…that one," answered Daniel.

"He told me his name was Paul Smith. He even had identification."

"Paul Smith, huh…you got an address?"

"Yeah, it's right there, on the proposal."

Daniel and Robney looked at the proposal, and then, without uttering another word, Daniel rose from his seat and rushed toward the exit.

"Why does that address look familiar?" asked Robney, rushing to catch up with Daniel.

"Because…that's my parent's old place!" exclaimed Daniel, while rushing passed the male receptionist.

# # #

34

Jeremy shuffled down the street knocking on doors, but no one, at the first five or six houses, opened up for him. However, when he came to the seventh house, the door opened and a young boy was standing behind the screen.

"Jeremy," said the boy, "My daddy told me not to give you anymore food. He said if I keep feeding you, you'll keep coming back."

"Uh…That ain't why I'm here…Uh, what I mean is…Uh…"

"Jeremy, you've got to go…before my daddy finds out you're here."

Jeremy backed away from the door, and the little boy. He looked back, over his shoulder, at the sidewalk leading away from the house.

"Have you seen my dog?" he whimpered when he turned to face the boy again. His voice sounded like a child's.

"Jeremy, you're scaring me?"

"Okay…"

Jeremy walked to the end of the sidewalk, but when he got to the gate, he turned back around and shouted, "I WANT MY DOG!" Then he took off and ran down the sidewalk.

When he arrived at the end of the block, Jeremy stopped to catch his breathe. Leaning against a tree, he covered his face and cried. He closed his eyes and covered his ears with his hands, trying to block out the neighborhood sounds. But when he hears counting, Jeremy opened his eyes and looked down. Standing there, leaning against the other side of the tree, stood the child version of Jeremy, and he's counting.

"One...!"

"No! No! No!" cried Jeremy, knowing what comes next. He reached for the boy, but his hand passed right through the child's shoulder.

"Two...!"

"HEY—"

Jeremy moved closer to his younger self and jumped up and down, and waving his hands in the air, he tried to get the child's attention.

"—STOP COUNTING!" he shouted, but the Jeremy child ignores him.

"Three...!"

Jeremy looked around for help, but there wasn't anyone in the neighborhood, so all he could do was watch the events unfold as he remembered them.

When the Jeremy child tilted his head back, and looked up, Jeremy thought the boy had seen him. But instead, the boy pointed toward the sky and marveled at the clouds. Upon hearing the voices of the other children, Jeremy looked around for them, hoping he could tell them not to let the little boy go off by himself. He ran out in the street and yelled for them to come out of hiding.

"Don't let him go off by his self!" he shouted.

"Four...Five...!"

At the end of his count, the Jeremy child ran off and disappeared behind some hedges.

Jeremy was standing in the middle of the street, when the boy disappeared. He dropped to his knees, and ignoring the cars swerving to avoid hitting him, cried.

"Get your drunken ass out'ta the street, before you get killed!" one driver shouted as he sped passed Jeremy.

"Homeless fucker!" shouted another.

Jeremy, unaware of the danger he had placed himself in, sat in the middle of the street. When he felt a hand on his shoulder, he whipped his head around to see the little boy from the last house he had visited. The boy's father was standing out in the street, diverting traffic.

"Jeremy, are you okay?" asked the little boy, but when Jeremy looked at the boy, all he saw was his child self, so he smiled, thinking he had saved himself.

"Am I okay…? For get about me! Are you Okay?" Jeremy asked the little boy.

"Uh huh?" answered the little boy, confused by Jeremy's response. He grabbed him by his arm and said, "Here, let me help you up."

"I was worried about you," Jeremy tells the boy.

"Me? Why? You're the one sitting in the middle of the street."

After standing, Jeremy looked around and appeared as though he was lost.

"Where am I?" he asked, and the boy, looking at his father, said, "Daddy, he's confused and don't know where he is."

"That's because he's a crack head," replied the father, showing no compassion. "C'mon, just get him out of the street, so he doesn't get killed in front of our house."

The boy led Jeremy to the sidewalk, and the father shoved some money in his hand. Then he grabbed his son's hand and walked away.

"Bye!" Jeremy called out to the little boy, "And thanks!"

Roscoe, appearing out of thin air, ran up to Jeremy and rested his front paws on Jeremy's leg.

"Now that's what I call a hustle! You played them to the hilt. What they give you…a twenty?"

"Huh…?" replied Jeremy. He looked down at his hand, and when he saw the cash, he opened his clinched fist to see what the boy's father had given him. His eyes widened.

"It's a hundred dollar bill!", he said, answering the dog.

"A hundred… You're shit'n me!"

Jeremy held up the money, and realizing it was the most he's ever gotten at one time, clutched it tightly against his chest.

"So…what are we going to buy first? I'm hungry…Ain't you hungry? Let's go buy something to eat; one of them juicy hamburger steak sandwiches would be great! Ain't you hungry? Come'on, let's go buy something to eat."

Jeremy walked away. He didn't want food. He wanted more crack cocaine, so he could squelch the memories and nightmares.

"I need my medicine."

"Are you still gonna go house to house; to talk to the parents about their kids tagging your car?"

"I need my medicine, so stop being a pest."

"Okay! Okay! Shesh, don't cut my head off."

# # #

35

The lobby of the Skyline Airport Hotel was neat and clean, but it wasn't the Peachtree Plaza Hotel. When Louise walked in, she is greeted by Saul. He is wearing blue jeans and a sweat shirt, not what she expected. There is a ball cap pulled over his bald head too, and he seems anxious, as if he is trying to conceal his face.

Louise ignores her intuition, chalking it up to the fact that she's a cop's daughter and taught to suspect everyone.

"I left the contract in my car," said Saul, as he ushered Louise out of the lobby before anyone could see them together.

"I have to leave earlier than I thought," he added, "So I'm sorry if it seems I'm rushing you."

"That's okay...I understand."

When Louise walked out of the lobby, she saw a dark blue car with its motor running, parked in front of the hotel. When the driver got out of the car, he rushed to open the door for her.

"I hope you don't mind doing this in the car?" asked Saul, and Louise, despite hearing her inner voice scream *don't get in the car* she got in anyway.

Once he got inside, Saul opened his briefcase and pulled out a piece of paper. He handed it to Louise, along with a pen.

"I don't understand...What's this for?" asked Louise, when she saw the paper was blank.

"So you can write to your husband and father."

"Huh…?" replied Louise. She looked up and saw the driver holding a gun in her face.

"Saul—" she attempted, but when she looked at Saul, he punched her in the jaw and everything went black.

# # #

36

Louise opened her eyes. The room she's in is empty, except for an old bed. There is a small oil burning lamp sitting in the corner on the floor. She tried to get up, but found herself bound to the bed, so Louise tried to call out for help, but the duct tape covering her mouth prevented her from doing that. The only movement allowed was to raise her head. But when she raised her head, and looked down, Louise saw she was naked. All of her clothes had been removed and were lying on top of a heaping pile of other old clothes. When she looked around, Louise saw, lying next to her and scattered on the filthy bed, an assortment of sex toys; some were covered in dried blood.

Several hours later...

Saul and Tim walk into the room. Saul was carrying a bag of fast food, and a bottle of water.

"If you're thirsty and hungry...nod," he said, and Louise complied. "Good. If I remove the duct tape are you gonna scream?"

Louise shook her head nodded again, so Saul reached out and grabbed one end of the tape. He slowly pealed it back, but once enough had been removed, Louise screamed.

After quickly replacing the tape, Saul stood. He dug his hand down into his pocket and pulled out some cash, which he hands over to Tim.

"You just cost me twenty bucks," he said, and then, slapping Louise, adds, "So get this straight bitch, if you cooperate, this will go better for you. We'll feed you and give you water, but if you insist on acting a fool, you're gonna end up starving or dying from dehydration...your choice. Now, do you want something to eat and drink?"

After Louise nodded; Saul, believing she understood, removed the duct tape again.

"Now, ain't that better?" he asked, while offering a drink of the water.

"Go to hell," muttered Louise, while still accepting the water. When Tim holds a burger up to her mouth, she takes several greedy bites.

"How long have I been out?" she asked, while chewing loudly.

"Quite a while...guess I hit you harder than I thought," answered Saul.

"And those?" asked Louise, gesturing to the sex toys, particularly those covered in blood.

"Don't worry, that ain't your blood," answered Tim. He knocked the toys off the bed with one sweeping motion of his hand. "That blood's from our last playmate. She was virginal material, but I'm sure we won't have such a *'tight'* problem with you, will we?"

Tim winked at Saul, but then he quickly looked down at Louise.

"What does that suppose to mean?" she asked, and Tim said, "If you can handle old hoss here..." he slapped Saul on his back. "You ain't gonna have any problems taking any of those."

Louise looked passed Tim to see Saul had dropped his pants. He was now standing there, holding his pecker.

Tim turned and looked at Saul too. When he faced Louise again, he saw the excitement in her eyes. She wasn't afraid of them.

"Don't you worry lassie," he said, "You'll get the opportunity again, but for the time being, you only get to watch."

Tim faced Saul and dropped to his knees in front of him. Taking hold of Saul's penis, he inserted it into his mouth.

Revolted by the sight, Louise turned her head and vomited. After Tim finished with Saul, he stood.

"What do you intend on doing with me?" asked Louise.

"Isn't it obvious?" answered Saul.

"My husband is a cop. He doesn't have any money to pay off a ransom."

"This ain't about money, honey. This is about *'get-back'*."

"Get back? Revenge...?"

"Yeah, bitch...revenge!" interjected Tim. "...for all the wrongs done to us!"

"By who...Daniel?" Louise looked at Tim. His mouth was still moist and his lips red from the blowjob he had just given Saul. "He's the sweetest, kindest man I know. He wouldn't hurt a fly."

"Is that why you let me spank that ass? Cause he's sweet and kind?"

"So I screwed up," replied Louise, angrily.

Louise closed her eyes and bit down on her lips, because she knew Saul was right; she had cheated on Daniel for no reason, other than being horny.

"He's still a good man," she added. "Besides...what did he do that you two didn't deserve, huh?"

"Well, I don't even know your man...but I still hate him, because Saul hates him. It ain't him I'm after. It's your daddy that's got my goat."

"Daddy...?" A puzzled look came over Louise's face. "How does an old fag like you know my daddy?"

"You don't recognize me, huh?" asked Tim, pretending Louise had hurt his feelings. "Why...I used to be mayor of this lovely city, until your daddy testified at my trial. He took away everything I worked for, so he's got to pay."

"Daniel took the one love of my life from me," interjected Saul. "He could've had any girl he wanted, back when we were teenagers, but he went after the one I wanted. That's what he's paying for."

"Oh...for Christ sake, you're both lunatics!" cried Louise.

Saul rushed forward. He grabbed Louise by her throat, and while kneeling beside the bed, reached beneath the mattress for his knife.

"Insulting us ain't gonna help you any. I suggest you watch your tongue, before I cut it off."

The knife was pressed against Louise's cheek, so she could feel the cold of its steel. While Saul stared into Louise's eyes, she could see the anger and deep hatred he harbored for Daniel.

"You understand what I'm saying?" growled Saul.

"Uh-huh, I understand…please, I can't breathe."

Saul released his grip and Louise inhaled. She began to cry, because she believed she's going to be kill; along with Daniel and father too.

"Saul…," she cried, hoping to sway Saul. "Please don't do this."

"Bitch, don't be playing to his dick!" barked Tim, when he saw what Louise was trying to do. He pushed Saul out of the way, and with his face in Louise's, adds, "He and I been together for a long time. We watched over each others back, so ain't nothing you can say or offer that I can't take care of myself! Just play along, and maybe…maybe you'll come out of this alive. But your daddy, and your man, I don't hold out much hope for them."

"Saul…," pleaded Louise, but Tim, not wanting to hear any more, tore off another piece of duct tape and covered her mouth.

"Let's go and make that call," he said, looking at Saul, when he gets up off the bed.

# # #

37

The cell phone buzzed. When Daniel glanced down at it, he saw Louise's name.

"Louise…?" he said, and not waiting for a respond, asked, "Where are you?"

"She's with me…" replied a familiar voice. It was Saul.

When Daniel heard the voice from the past, he slammed his foot down on his brake pedal and brings his car to a skidding halt, but he didn't respond.

"Didn't you hear me? I said, 'She's with me'. And I think she's enjoying herself."

"Saul…" whispered Daniel, "What have you done? Where is my wife?"

"I told you…she's with me!"

Saul sounded cheery, and seemed genuinely happy that he was speaking with an old friend.

"She came to me this morning and let me fuck her brains out, and she must've wanted more, because she came back this evening."

"Why are you doing this?"

While Daniel questioned Saul, Robney called the operator to have the phone call traced.

"This is Detective Morris of the Atlanta PD…" he said, whispering into his phone. "My badge number is 052659. I need you to trace a cell phone call. This is an emergency!"

"Yes sir!" responded the operator. When Robney looked at Daniel, he placed a hand over his phone and whispered, "Keep 'em talking."

Daniel nodded, understanding.

"You hear me Saul, why are you doing this?" he asked, and Saul lets out a frightening laugh.

"You want to speak to your wife?" he asked, and the holding the phone next to Louise's head, said, "Here…" But when Louise didn't say anything, he growled, "Say something!"

Daniel heard Louise moan passionately.

"Louise? Baby, are you alright?"

"I'd say she's doing better than alright," answered Saul. He had pulled the phone away from Louise, and held it up to his own ear. He chuckled too, because Tim was working a massive dildo in and out of Louise's twat.

"Yeah, I'd say she's having the time of her life."

"Saul!" shouted Daniel, "I'm gonna kill you!"

"You know Daniel…you've never changed, have you? You're always making promises you can't keep."

Daniel slammed his hand against his steering wheel, and he gripped the cell phone he held so tightly that Robney thought he was going to break it.

"Man," said Daniel, through clinched teeth. "What have I done to deserve this? What has my wife done to deserve this?"

Saul reached over and ripped the duct tape off Louise's mouth, and she lets out a blood curdling screamed. While it seemed to Daniel she was in a great deal of pain; had he of been there, he would have seen she was, in fact, experiencing a powerful orgasm.

"Hear that?" asked Saul. "That ain't because she's hurting…if you get my drift."

"What's that suppose to mea—" began Daniel, but he stopped talking, because just before the phone went dead, he heard Louise cry, "Please, don't stop…!"

Sitting there, with his mouth open, Daniel didn't know what to think or say. When he turned his head and looked at Robney, the detective shook his head back and forth.

"There wasn't enough time to trace the call," said Robney, but then he asked, "What did he say? Did he let you talk to your wife?"

Daniel nods, but he didn't reveal any details. Instead, Daniel puts his car in gear and drives on.

#

"Now it's my turn," said Tim. He pulled the dildo out of Louise, and handed it to Saul. He took the cell phone and began scrolling through Louise's address book, until he found Darryl's name. He presses the *send* button and waited.

#

Darryl was pacing his office when he received the call from Louise's cell phone.

"Louise, honey?" he asks, sounding relieved, but then came a familiar laugh.

"Darryl, me boy…how the hell are you?"

"Tim, have you lost your fucken mind…killing all of those innocent girls?"

"Well…I thought you'd be more concerned about your daughter, but here you are, worried about hookers again."

"This is my city, so I'm concerned about everyone's safety. You use to think that way, what happened to you?"

"What happened to me? What happened to me?" repeated Tim. "I spent the past ten years locked in a six by twelve cell sucking dick and being ass fucked by the biggest, blackest, son-of-a-bitch I'd ever seen in my entire life! That's what happened to me!"

"And somehow this is my fault? You decided abducting my daughter is the way to make me pay, right? Well, that's smart."

"Listen here lad'die, the last thing you want to do right now is *PISS ME OFF*!"

Tim hung up the phone. When he saw Saul giving Louise some more water he barked, "What the hell do you think you're doing?" and Saul looked up.

"Huh?"

"Don't give that bitch anything, you hear me? I want her to suffer."

"Tim," said Saul as he backed away from the bed. "I done told you about miss directing your anger toward me, haven't I? Now we agreed to kill Daniel and Darryl, but we ain't said nothing about killing Louise."

"What…you going soft on me? Hell…we done killed so many bitches; one more ain't gonna make a difference."

Saul glanced down at Louise, and agreeing with Tim, shrugged. He sat the bottle of water on the floor and re-taped her mouth shut.

"Sorry babe, but he's right."

# # #

38

Darryl slammed the cell phone down, realizing he's probably sentenced his daughter to death. But instead of letting his emotions take over, he embraced his training and picked up his desk phone.

"I just got a call from my daughter's cell phone. I want you to backtrack it."

"Is the caller still on the line?"

"No, but her phone has GPS. If it's still powered up, you should be able to get a location on it. I'm sending you the ID code now."

Darryl typed the codes into an email message and pressed the send button. But when the female operator said, "Give me a couple of minutes," he barked, "I ain't got a couple of minutes!"

"Yes sir, I'm working as quickly as I can."

Darryl sighed, and realizing he was taking his anger out on the operator, he said, "Thank you," and hung up the phone. But just as quickly as he hung it up, he reached for his cell. This time, he called Daniel.

"I just spoke with Tim, and he's got Louise."

"I know…I just got off the phone with Saul."

"Got any leads? Anything…?"

"We got an address from Saul's P.O. That's were we're headed to right now."

"Okay…good. Maybe that asshole was dumb enough to give a real address."

"Yeah...well, it is a real address. I should know, because I lived there for the first eighteen years of my life."

"What?"

"Those fuckers are messing with our heads, captain."

"Well, I've got techs tracking down Louise's phone. It has a GPS tracking system in it. I'll call you once I get an address."

"Okay Captain," said Daniel, and then he adds, "And Dad...Don't worry, we'll find her."

"I know..." answered Darryl, and he hangs up the phone.

When they walk out of their hideout, Saul headed toward the end of the cul-de-sac, where Daniel's old home was located. They walked to the back of the house; where Saul kicked open the kitchen door. He tossed Louise's cell inside.

"Why'd you do that?"

"She's a cop's daughter, so her phone's probably lowjacked with a GPS system."

"Yeah, but why place the phone in your buddy's old house?"

"Just another way for me to fuck with him, like the roses. Now come on, let's go get something to eat."

Jeremy was walking down the street, sucking on a crack pipe. He occasionally stopped and stood in place; not caring if anyone saw him.

"You know, one of these days that shits gonna kill you."

"Yeah, but today ain't that day."

"I'm hungry."

"I ain't hungry, so shut up and come on."

"Where are we going?"

"Back to our house, where else?"

"But...? We're going in the wrong direction."

Roscoe stopped walking. He turned his head and looked back, in the direction they had come.

"We're going the wrong way!"

Jeremy pauses on a corner and lit his pipe again. After taking a draw from it, he stepped out into the street and is nearly struck by a passing blue car.

"Hey, I'm walking here!"

As the car zooms pass Jeremy, he sees the driver's face and recognizes him. He dropped the crack pipe and lighter he's holding, and while standing in the middle of the street, watches the car, until it turns a corner.

"I told you that shit was going to get you killed!"

The dog had been several paces behind Jeremy, and after the car sped by, he ran up to Jeremy.

"Are you alright?"

Jeremy doesn't react to the dog's concern. Instead, he begins to walk after the blue car.

"Slow down!" shouts Tim. "You're gonna kill somebody!"

"I thought you said killing one more don't matter?" replied Saul, driving recklessly.

"I didn't mean people walking down the street. You know they're looking for us, so it would be stupid to get busted for a traffic violation...wouldn't it?"

Saul slowed the car in response to Tim's questions. He glanced up and looked into his rear view mirror, where he saw a man spinning around in the street.

"That was just a crack head."

###

39

Daniel and Robney sat quietly on the porch of his childhood home and watched, while SWAT exited their tactical van and rushed toward the house.

When Darryl walked up to the porch, Daniel held out Louise's cell phone.

"It was lying on the floor in the kitchen," he said and stood. As Darryl stepped forward, and was about to enter the house, Daniel placed his hand on his shoulder and stopped him.

"She ain't in there, so don't go getting yourself all worked up."

"I ain't getting myself worked up," snapped Darryl, and it was obvious to Daniel that he was struggling with his emotions.

Darryl stared at the house for a moment, but then turned and walked away. When he got to his car, he called to Daniel and said, "Find her…please!"

Robney stood and watched Darryl's car, until it turned the corner. After that, he turned to Daniel.

"Are you okay?"

"Yeah," replied Daniel. He walked back into the house and stood in the middle of the empty living room. "You know, that mother fucker used to come to my house to eat all the time."

Daniel turned and faced Robney.

"If he hurts her…" he added, "I swear, I'm gonna turn my shield in and take it to the next level."

"And I'm with you all the way...partner."

#

Driving out of the neighborhood, empty handed, was like crawling out of the ocean after swimming against the tide for several grueling hours. When Daniel came to a halt at the corner, he glanced at the empty house sitting on the corner. It still looked haunted.

"What?" asked Robney, when he looked from Daniel to the house. "What's wrong?"

"Nothing," answered Daniel, as he drove on pass the house.

"So what's the plan now?"

Daniel shrugs and said, "I don't know...We wait, I guess."

"Wait? For what...?"

"For those two lunatics to make a mistake, and they will."

"How do you figure that? Up until now, they've covered their tracks perfectly."

"Because, I know Saul...He's one arrogant bastard and he thinks he can muscle his way through everything, and everybody, but I was always smarter. So I'm gonna figure out his next move, and then, I'm gonna bust him, if it's the last thing I do."

#

The taco stand was busy. When Jeremy arrived there, he stood on the corner, across the street from it, and waited.

Look at him, he thought, while watching Saul. Eating and acting as though he didn't do anything; stuffing his face like he deserves nutrition.

Tim talked while he ate, but he stopped, when he saw Jeremy standing on the corner watching them.

Once Jeremy realized Tim had noticed him watching, he began to pretend he was quarterbacking a football game.

Tim chuckled and resumed eating, when Jeremy started pretending.

"What?" Saul asked. He turned and looked at Jeremy too.

"I know him from somewhere, but I can't put a finger on the face."

"That's the homeless dude you almost ran over," commented Tim just as he bit down on the taco he held.

"I don't know...there's something else about him that seems familiar."

Saul stared at Jeremy, until he decides he doesn't know him. Facing Tim, he finished his meal.

#

After throwing his trash away, Saul walked over to his car, but before getting in, he stared at Jeremy once more.

"Damn, I know I know him from somewhere..."

"Com'on man, let's get back to the house. I don't feel comfortable out in the open like this."

"You ain't got nothing to worry 'bout," said Saul. He turned away from Jeremy and looked at Tim. "This here is my hood, and I rule here."

#

"Keep playing!" Jeremy mumbled to himself. "Just keep playing and he'll go away!"

"What is your crazy ass talk'n 'bout now, and what's that you're doing?"

"I'm playing football! Don't you know anything?"

"Football...? Looks like you're practicing to scratch somebody else's balls to me."

"Oh, just shut up and let me know when they leave."

The dog whipped its head around, trying to see who Jeremy was talking about, but it falls off. After re-attaching it, and looking up, it sees Saul and Tim getting into their car.

"Hey, aren't those the fuckers who almost ran us down?"

"Five twenty-six...hut, hut, hut!" shouts Jeremy. After taking the imaginary football from the imaginary center, Jeremy backs up and then, pretends to heave the ball into the sky. He stopped moving, mimicking the *perfect* release, and then runs after the ball. Jeremy leaps into the air and catches the football. When he lands, he tucks it into the crux of his arm and runs down the street, weaving pass a gang of imaginary defensive players, until he crosses his imaginary goal line. He raises his hands triumphantly, slams the imaginary football against the ground and dances a victory jig.

"They're gone now! Let's go over there and dig around in the garbage can for food?"

"No…we need to follow them."

# # #

40

Daniel parked in the precinct parking lot and shut off the ignition, but he didn't open the door of his car to get out. Instead, he sat there, staring forward.

"Are you coming in?"

Robney had already opened his door and was about to get out.

"I can't face him. I can't just go in there and look into that old man's eyes, and tell him I've run out of leads."

Robney closed his door and said, "Okay, then let's go get a drink."

Daniel started the car again, but instead of heading to their usual watering hole, he drove back the way he had come.

"Where you going?" asked Robney, but Daniel only shook his head; something was bothering him.

"Saul placed the phone in my old house," he said.

"Yeah, so…that's right…So what…?"

"The address Tim gave that P.O. was my old house and the roses…Saul wants me to find him. He wants me to know where he's hiding."

"And where would that be?" asked Robney, pushing Daniel. "He's been in prison for the past ten years, and he lived on the west coast for several years prior to that, so where would he hide in his old stomping ground?"

"He'd go to familiar surroundings like…Like his old club house!"

Daniel stomped down on the accelerator and the car's wheel's squealed in response.

"That old boarded up house down the street from my parent's house. That's were he is!"

#

When Jeremy arrived at the house, he stood in the street and stared at it. It still looked haunted, but no longer scared, he walked around the back and saw the blue car.

#

"Stop crying bitch!" barked Tim, while he raped Louise for the third time.

"Get up man, she can't take no more!" cried Saul, and when he tries to physically move Tim, Tim pushes him back.

"You're acting as though she was the one who booted you out of office."

"She's his daughter and that's enough for me—" replied Tim, but when he heard a noise, he tilted his head and stopped talking.

"Hear that?" he asked, "Someone's in the house."

Saul looked toward the open doorway, and all he could see beyond it was the dark hallway.

"Ain't nobody there," he said, "All the kids in this neighborhood think this place is haunted, which is why I chose it."

"I tell ya', I heard something. Go check it out!"

Saul put on his jeans, and barefooted, he tip-toed up to the door. He turned his head to one side and listened. When he didn't hear anything, Saul walked out and stood in the hall, but he didn't see anything either. He crept down the hall, peeking into the other rooms along the way, but saw nothing.

After walking back to the back bedroom, Saul stuck his head back in through the open door

"Must've been the wind—" he began, but stopped talking abruptly, when he heard giggling.

"That ain't the wind," whispered Tim, "Go check it out."

Saul walked away without saying a word and disappeared into the darkness. As he ventured down the hallway, Saul didn't see Jeremy pressed against a wall. Nor did he see the knife he held.

When Saul felt the knife stab into his lower back, he reached back to touch the spot where the pain emanated from. When he raised his hand, Saul couldn't see the blood covering it, but he can tell from the sticky texture what it is.

"What the—" he moans, but before Saul can finish speaking, Jeremy grabbed him from behind and yanked back his head, and he cuts his throat from ear to ear.

"Saul!" called Tim. He was still in the bedroom with Louise. Saul opened his mouth, and tried to warn Tim, but all he could manage was a bloody gurgle.

"Saul…" called Tim, again. But this time he was standing just inside the room, staring at the open door. "Are you out there?"

Tim moved closer to the door. He leaned forward and peered into the dark hallway, trying to see what was there. But, because there was no light and no shadows, he didn't see Jeremy thrusting the knife toward him. It entered his head up through Tim's chin.

#

41

Daniel's tires skidded to a halt in front of the old house. He and Robney leapt out of the car and rushed up the steps, and without hesitation, they kicked open the door. With flashlights in hand, the detectives moved forward slowly; searching. When they came upon Saul's body, Robney flipped him over. His head had been nearly taken off. There was a rose lying next to him.

When they discovered Tim's naked body lying in an open bedroom doorway, Robney and Daniel planted their bodies on both sides of the door. When they looked into the room, they saw Jeremy. He was sitting on the bed and holding his blade against Louise's neck. She was weeping, but he was grinning madly.

"Jerry," said Daniel, and he walked into the room. "Put the knife down."

"You were supposed to protect me! I'm your little brother! You're supposed to look out for me!"

Daniel stepped over Tim's body and tried to approach the bed, but Jeremy, warning him, pressed the knife against Louise's neck. The blade cut into her soft skin and blood began to spray out of her wound.

"Jerry...No!" cried Daniel. He held up his weapon and kneeling, laid it on the floor.

"Look, I'm unarmed...Jerry, think about what it is you're doing."

"I have thought about what I've done."

A puzzled expression came to Daniel's face, because he didn't know what Jeremy was talking about.

"Jerry, what are you talking about? What have you done?"

"What have I done? You know what I've done."

"Jerry, com'on…Let's go home and talk about it, just don't hurt my wife. Please…"

"You care more 'bout her than me, don't 'cha?"

"No…that's not it. It's just—"

"And you cared about them whores' more'n you cared 'bout me too, didn't you?"

"Jeremy, what are you talking about? What whores?"

"T-t-there was t-that n-nurse whore…I s-saw you go into her house. Y-you stayed there all n-night. I saw y-you creep out, like a t-thief too…like you s-stole something."

"Who are you—" began Daniel, but then he remembered the nights he had spent with Terrie, and her murder.

"Jerry, what did you do?"

"I couldn't have her t-telling folk m-my brother s-stole from her, so I p-put her down."

"God…no!" cried Daniel, when he realized he had been tracking the wrong person all along.

"And those whore s-sisters…t-they tried to get me to *'do'* it with t-them, right after t-they had f-finished *'doing'* that other guy. Said t-they n-needed more, so I gave 'em what I had…m-my blade."

"God, Daniel he's the rose killer," whispered Robney, but Daniel quickly held up his hand, gesturing for Robney to shut up.

"I got this," he said, and then facing Jeremy again, said, "Jerry, why are you doing this?"

"Because, I'm your little brother and you're supposed to watch out for me…but you didn't."

Jeremy's voice tapered off and he begins to weep.

"Saul took away my innocence, right here in this room, and you didn't do anything to stop him."

"Jerry, I didn't know."

"I tried to tell you, but he was there, watching me."

"Jerry, I didn't know."

"And he kept raping me, until I was ten years old."

"Please Jerry...I didn't know. But look, he's dead now, so you don't have to be afraid if him anymore."

Jeremy saw Robney standing in the shadows, and he saw the gun he aimed at him. He knew he was not going to leave the room; ever again.

"He's gonna do her," whispered Robney as he cocked his revolver, and was preparing to fire. "Look in his eyes man, he's gonna do her!"

"SHUT UP!" barked Daniel, and he turned his head and looked back. When he turned back to face Jeremy, Daniel saw him move the blade away from Louise's neck.

"NO-O-O-O-O!" cried Daniel as Jeremy moved the blade across his own neck.

Daniel rushed forward and caught Louise, just as she fell forward. He pressed his palm against her wound and tried to slow the bleeding, but because of that, Daniel wasn't able to help Jeremy.

Robney put his gun away and rushed around the bed, but he was too late to save Jeremy.

"I'm sorry man, he's gone."

"I know..." replied Daniel, sadly. He looked up, over the bed, to where Robney was standing. "Please call a bus for my wife, okay?"

"Yeah, okay..." replied Robney, and then he walked out of the room and out of the house, where he received a better signal on his cell phone.

"This is Officer Morris; send a bus over to..."

###

EPILOGUE

In the hospital room; Daniel slumbered in the chair next to Louise's bed. He dreamt of the boy, but this time, the boy smiled warmly at him, instead of haunting him. When he waved good bye, Daniel opened his eyes and turned to find Louise had been watching him. He sat up in his chair.

"I'm supposed to be watching over you," said Daniel and Louise smiled.

"The boy's gone, isn't he?" she asked.

"How'd you know?" answered Daniel, with a slight nod of his head.

"Because I've been laying here watching you for hours, and that's the longest I've ever known you to sleep. So I figured he had to be gone, otherwise you'd be up; pacing the floor."

Daniel smiled. He stood and leaning over the bed, lightly kisses Louise on her forehead. When he pulled back, and was about to sit back down, Louise grabbed Daniel and pulled him closer.

"Daniel, there's something I need to tell you."

"No…no there isn't," replied Daniel, reassuringly. "Just know that I love you and I'm sorry to have involved you in this mess."

"But—" said Louise as she stared sadly into Daniel's tired eyes.

Daniel smiled and tried to comfort his traumatized wife. He rubbed his hand over her forehead, ever so gently.

"Louise, I love you…" he said, "Do you love me?"

"Yes, with all my heart."

"Then that's all you need to tell me."

"But…"

"Shush, now go back to sleep. You need the rest, doctor's orders. And don't worry; I'll be here when you wake up. I'll always be here."

Louise, weeping, closed her eyes and fell back to sleep, knowing Daniel loved her and that he would never leave her side.

# # #

THE END

Other books by Davied E. Kelley, Jr.

A SON RISING IN THE WEST
A SON DOWN IN THE SOUTH

CPSIA information can be obtained at www.ICGtesting.com
225050LV00002B/20/P

9 781456 024901